JESSICA LYNCH

HOUSE OF CARDS

ROYAL ANGELS

FORGED IN TWILIGHT BOOK ONE

FORGED IN TWILIGHT

House of Cards is my first entry in a brand new interlinked series of novellas. It's based in an alternate world—full of factions and paranormal beings—separate from my *Claws Clause* series, though it features the same type of paranormal characters you love from my other PNR books. In this novella, I'm writing about a trio of angel princes who are searching for their talisman—and luck on their fated soulmates.

The *Forged in Twilight* series is an out-of-this-world magical experience featuring a collection of seven different paranormal romance authors.

My set of three novellas will be set in Las Vegas, Nevada—Sin City itself—and will feature characters that you'll meet in some of the other authors' books.

So, go on. Enjoy the angst, romance, action, love, and—of course—*magic* in the *Forged in Twilight* series:

Angels: House of Cards by Jessica Lynch
Vampires: Forged in Blood by P.T. Macias
Demons: Guardian's Spell by Kimila Taylor
Dragons: Breathing Fire by Alexi Ferreira
Fae: Claimed by the Fae Prince by Ember-Raine Winters
Phoenix: Ensnared in Flames by Angel Nyx
Bears: Wicked Treason by Lia Davis

FORGED IN TWILIGHT
PARANORMAL ROMANCE

PROLOGUE

The air smelled of fire and brimstone.

It didn't take a werewolf's nose to scent it on the edge of twilight, but the stink had hit Dane as he loped through the forest in his two-legged form; tall and muscular, he was a dark shadow amongst the trees. He stopped short, snuffling as he pawed at his face, trying to force the burning scent from his nose, but it was so overpowering that he resigned himself from trying. Frustration had his golden eyes flaring—or maybe that was the reflection of the bright orange flames filtering in through a break in the closely grown trees.

Stealth was the werewolf's friend. Earlier, when he caught sight of Lucifer—the Morningstar himself— pacing nearby instead of his own realm down below, Dane was curious. It wasn't often that Lucifer was caught out of his realm of Hell, especially in this corner of the world.

So, rather than moving on and continuing with his own hunt that night, he followed behind Lucifer at a distance, keeping the other male in sight as he remained undetected.

Everyone who identified as one of the paranormal factions in their world would recognize Lucifer at first glance. A couple of inches taller than Dane—who, at 6'2", was no slouch—with that swarthy goatee, piercing ice-cold blue eyes, and shoulder-length black hair he habitually wore tied back at the nape of his neck with a strip of dark leather, Lucifer stood out. Add that to the aura of Hell that cloaked him and... yeah. Dane followed.

Was it smart? Probably not. But Dane was curious, and though he was careful to stay out of sight, he realized that Lucifer had reasons of his own to be out at twilight when he smelled the fire, saw the flickering orange light against the dark bark of the nearby trees, and found the source of the brimstone.

A forge. There was a forge set up in a clearing just past the copse of trees where Dane was hiding.

Lucifer had been pacing before; a hint of nerves had eked out from under the overwhelming sulfurous odor clinging to the intimidating male. Now? He was exuding a mixture of confidence and determination that had Dane's wolf side bristling.

Something wasn't right—and it had everything to do with the forge.

Time to go, he thought. Nothing Lucifer was doing could be good, and if he was using fire straight out of the pits of Hell—because what else had fed his forge? —then Dane needed to get the hell out of there before Lucifer sicced it on him.

But, before Dane could use his innate stealth to sneak off undetected, Lucifer threw back his head. The flames rose high in the forge, the point of his goatee shining with the blaze of the fire in front of him. Dane's position threw Lucifer's wickedly beautiful profile in sharp relief as he planted his leather boots against the earth.

Then, his strong stance vibrating in power, he lifted his hands as the lord of Hell began a throaty chant that had Dane frozen in place—

"Forged in twilight, cursed by fire,
powers of each divided by my ire.
Sever them in three,
one to true love it will be.
One to the nearest object the curse will keep,
the last with the beings,
the power will sleep..."

As the wind picked up, Lucifer's chant landing like a smith's hammer against an iron anvil, Dane burrowed deeper among the trees, suddenly extremely eager to stay hidden. Curiosity was one thing; drawing attention to his spying was something else entirely, especially since he was *spying* on *Lucifer*.

There was dark magic at work here. The stink of sulfur—rotten eggs that had his stomach tightening—was bad enough, but the bitter edge kept him from turning tail and running.

Or maybe that was Lucifer's palpable fury, the weight of every word in his ominous chant keeping Dane lurking just out of his sight, fighting the pull to stay and listen while his wolf's survival instincts snapped at him to *run*—

> "Forged in fire and light,
> bringing all beings' powers together
> to be *put* to *right*—"

With that final word, Dane's muscular body jerked. As something deep inside of him was being ripped out through his chest, he unscrewed his jaw enough to let loose a growl of pain—but the echo of Lucifer's curse was all he heard. The snarl strangled in his throat, his oversized canines clicking together as his mouth clamped shut.

It was dark. The air smelled of fire and brimstone and *agony* as Dane's knees buckled, his big body hitting the ground hard as he dropped to the dirt, like a tree after it had been felled by an ax.

No one was around to yell 'timber' as Dane keeled over, but if there had been? Not even a werewolf's impressive hearing would've caught it as the effect of Lucifer's targeted curse tore through him, stealing some of his soul—and the last of his consciousness, too.

CHAPTER 1

"**W**here's Sam?"

At his eldest brother's bark, Micah jerked his head up from the device he was fiddling with.

Stubborn to a fault, Micah just couldn't accept that, as an angel, his celestial aura meant that every single electronic toy he played with would be shorted out as soon as he got his angelic hands on it. And, sure, they could pay one of the other more magically-inclined factions to ward his gizmos and gadgets like they did with everything else the brothers relied on to succeed in the human world, but... *stubborn*. Micah was convinced that he could figure it out on his own if he just kept at it.

Which was fine. Raze didn't give a shit what his youngest brother did during his downtime. But when it was near the hour when their casino really started to get crowded and Samael had conveniently pulled another disappearing act, he had less patience than usual.

Micah ran his fingers through his light brown hair, brow furrowed as he met the glare in Raze's steely blue gaze. With a shrug, he admitted, "Don't know, Raze. He said he was going out last night and he hasn't come back yet."

"Did you call him?"

Beneath his tanned complexion, his youngest brother paled. He picked up the device he'd been playing with again.

This time, Raze recognized it as Micah's personal cell phone.

And it was *smoking*.

"Seriously? Wasn't that warded?"

"I had Hilda take the spell off," Micah said defiantly. Hilda was the serious, spell-obsessed manager of the local Twilight Café. She was also a witch who had a bit of a sweet spot when it came to Micah. "I really want to make this work. Especially with the way our auras are... you know. I thought I could use my phone without it exploding on me."

You know... yeah. Raze did. And while their auras had taken a hit over the last few years, it was good to see that they were still powerful enough to short out an electronic—even if Micah couldn't see the benefit in retaining some of their God-given powers.

"Get that fixed," Raze ordered.

"Yes, sir."

Smartass.

Raze was just about to offer his brother a well-deserved retort when, suddenly, the door to their office pushed slowly open. While the brothers each had suites of their own near the top of the Twilight Sphere hotel, their office was a shared space off of the back half of their casino. Only four souls were allowed entrance. The three owners—Raze, Sam, and Micah—plus Cael, another fallen angel who had been their trusted floor manager since House of Sin first opened.

Even though he was a respected member of their team, Cael still averted his silvery gaze as he approached the two brothers. In his hand, he held another—thankfully *not* smoking—cell phone. As he crossed the room, he zeroed in on Raze.

"Phone for you, boss."

"Micah can handle it. It's warded, so he should be fine."

Rolling his eyes while plopping the useless device he was still holding onto back on his cluttered desk, Micah offered his palm out to Cael.

But the floor manager didn't drop it. Instead, with an apologetic grimace pulling his cherubic face, he held it out to Raze. "They asked for you special."

Of course they did.

"This better not have something to do with Sam," he muttered, taking the phone from Cael.

The middle prince was nothing but trouble most of the time. While they were still ascended angels, Samael had been one of the favored. Though he hadn't been quite as powerful as an archangel, he was an angel of death—at least, he *used* to be. Ever since the brothers were cast out of Heaven millennia ago, he got this idea that he could earn them a return trip back to the celestial cities if only he used his powers for good. As a self-professed guardian angel, he'd prove that Michael himself made a mistake by punishing Raze and Micah when it was Sam who was really the one to blame.

Raze gave up trying to convince his stubborn brother that it wasn't his fault shortly after they fell. He knew that it was their talisman—a golden key that opened the pearly gates of Heaven—going missing that kept the angels out of their former home. But since it had been missing for just as long as they'd been trapped in Purgatory, Sam couldn't help but believe that saving enough lives—after being responsible for taking countless—would replace their missing key.

It wouldn't, but at least it gave Sam purpose.

Or, it had—until Polly Benson.

Raze scowled. When it came to Sam's fixation with

that human thief of his, he wished his brother would go back to acting like any other soul's guardian angel.

Some of the factions mingled with the humans. Raze preferred not to if he could avoid it, but with the success of their casino, he'd discovered that a mortal's cash was just as good as a paranormal being's; he wasn't going to discriminate just because they were short-lived and magic-free. So long as the humans were willing to spend, he was willing to take their money, and the business-minded Raze left it at that.

House of Sin was still a faction-owned and operated facility. Located on the third floor of the Twilight Sphere hotel in the heart of the City of Sin, Raze opened their doors to anyone, though a majority of their customers were paranormal; his staff was completely faction, mostly angel, with shifters, witches, sirens, and other beings reporting to his management team.

The casino wasn't the only faction-run building in the hotel. There was the Twilight Bar & Grille, the Twilight Nights Club, the Café, and the Twilight Sweets Bakery owned by a curvy fairy named Rhea and her petite demoness partner, Ariel.

Speaking of Ariel—

Taking the phone from Cael, Raze snapped his name. "Raze speaking."

"Raze. Hi. It's me. Ariel. You know... from the bakery?"

Though he wasn't a big dessert guy, Ariel was a whizz when it came to making cupcakes. She also had a way with a paintbrush. He actually had one of her paintings hanging in his living room up in his suite. When he commissioned it from her, he'd offered her as much money as she wanted, but she wasn't interested in monetary payment. Proving she learned very well from her fairy partner, Ariel requested a favor instead.

"Let me guess," he drawled. "This is about your favor."

"You got it."

That was fine with Raze. He hadn't liked being in debt to anyone, especially—if he was being honest—a demoness. Ariel was born that way, so she belonged to the demon faction instead of being one of Lucifer's, but still. He was an angel, and some prejudices died hard.

"Whatever it is, you got it."

"Now, I know that you said the favor's not transferable, so I understand if you won't help her, but I've got this friend. A pretty redhead who's in need. She's convinced the only one who can help her is an angel and, I thought, I know a guy. If anyone can do what she needs, it's Raze."

As if he wasn't already aggravated with his two brothers, now this. Turning away from Cael and Micah, he said gruffly into the warded phone, "What is it she needs from me?"

"Well, that's really her story to tell."

"Then I don't see—"

"Five minutes," chirped Ariel in her high-pitched voice. "That's all I'm asking for. She's going to be down at the Twilight Bar at seven tonight. She's a real redhead, but I don't think you can miss her anyway. Talk to her for five minutes, see what she has to say, and that's your favor. Deal?"

A deal with a demoness? Well, it was better than owing a favor.

"Fine," he relented. "Tell your friend I'll meet her at seven. She gets five minutes of my time and that's your favor done."

He could hear the way she was beaming through her words as she said, "Ah. You're the best, Raze."

"Yeah, yeah."

He hung up the phone, passing it back to Cael.

"What was that about?" asked Micah.

"That was Ariel."

"From the bakery?"

How many Ariels did he know? "Yeah. She has a friend who wants a favor from an angel. I'll give her five minutes, then head out to the casino. See if you can track down Sam, and I'll meet you on the floor. Okay?"

"Sounds good, Raze."

"Oh. And Micah?"

"Yeah?"

"Try not to blow up any more phones."

Micah shot him his middle finger. Even from across the desk, Raze noticed the patch of shiny, raw skin where the phone must've burned him after it shorted out. Angels were immortal; their healing abilities almost as impressive as a shifter's. The fact that the mark was still there was another truth he wanted to avoid.

Great. Fucking *great*.

With a wave over at Micah and a nod toward Cael, Raze headed toward the back entrance of the office. There was an executive elevator in the hall, one that would take him anywhere in the hotel without having to step out into the hustle and bustle of the casino's floor.

House of Sin was open around the clock, though Raze never went out on the floor until nighttime when it was the busiest; it was only then that the benefits outweighed his annoyance at the noise. The jolt of the patrons worshipping the one-eyed bandit gave his waning powers a much needed boost, so he'd make his appearance before retreating to his suite alone.

But, first, the favor.

Ariel said that her friend would be down at one of the hotel's bars at seven o'clock. He would stop in then, give her the five minutes he promised Ariel, then get on with his night.

It seemed like a good enough plan to Raze. Micah

was tasked with locating Sam, so at least he didn't have to worry about that. Still, an emissary from the vampire faction in the City of Souls—a faction-based community in London—was supposed to be visiting the casino tonight. Another chore he could delegate if he wanted to, but he should make sure the servers had chilled blood on hand just in case.

It was the little touches that made him feel like he was involved in running the casino instead of just profiting off of its patrons.

He needed their adoration like a fix. Their money, too. Ever since the three of them had fallen, Raze had made it his goal to ascend again. Until then, though, he wanted to be comfortable. His obscene wealth made that possible.

In fact, he wanted for nothing.

And he believed that until the clock struck seven and, punctual as ever, he walked into the darkness of the Twilight Bar and Grille—and immediately stopped.

Before he stepped foot inside of the bar, he would've sworn that he never noticed the emptiness in his chest. Then he did, and it was as if he was a balloon being pumped full of air. His heart stuttered, and there was a tug deep in his soul that had his gaze torn right toward the most beautiful woman he'd ever seen before in his life.

Ivory skin. Pale eyes. And blood-red hair that

couldn't be real, but that he sensed undoubtedly was, just like Ariel had said.

That wasn't the only thing he sensed, either.

His angelic aura started pinging the way it always did when a demon was near. Not only that, but his cock twitched before starting to harden. Within seconds, he was completely erect and totally uncomfortable as the bulge pushed against his business slacks.

He was instantly aroused—and it was all because of *her*.

His soulmate.

It was his *soulmate*.

The one soul meant for him, the one soul he'd managed to avoid coming across for so long. Now, after thousands of years, he'd finally stumbled upon her.

And, unless he was mistaken—and Raze was positive he wasn't—she was the friend that Ariel had convinced him to meet with.

Holy fucking hell.

Five minutes would never be enough.

CHAPTER 2

Becca Murphy had been sitting at her table for more than two hours in the hopes that Ariel would come through for her. With every minute that passed, she had to work to convince herself not to bolt before the angel appeared. In fact, she had purposely arrived early because, if she hadn't, odds were she'd totally wimp out.

But she couldn't. As soon as she confessed her intentions to Ariel, a fellow demoness, she'd already done the one thing she knew she never should: she betrayed Lucifer.

She needed the angel's help or she was totally fucked.

Nerves stole her appetite; the sweet human server with the blonde ponytail and kind smile served her a basket of fresh-baked bread that she nibbled on, and a glass of water spiked with lemon that Becca anxiously sipped. The Twilight Bar & Grille located inside of the infamous Twilight Sphere hotel in Sin City, Las Vegas —or, as the paranormal beings all called it, the City of Sin—was known for its food and its drink as well as the werewolves who owned and operated it.

She'd never been inside before. It was nice, if definitely dark. The walls were a rich purple with silver accents, the bar itself made of gleaming black wood with a white pearl granite countertop. Becca was sitting at a tall table—black with matching high-top stools— near the back of the bar, people-watching and waiting for Raziel.

Working down in Hell, spending the last few years in the Pit... it must've driven her crazy. Why else would she have thought turning to Raziel—the eldest of the Angels of Sin City—for help was a good idea?

Then again, it was the only one she had. She just hoped that the leverage she brought with her would be enough to engage his aid otherwise Becca was looking at her second and final death.

The first one hadn't been so bad. She'd made it to the ripe old age of eighty-six before Lucifer came calling in her debt. After a foolhardy mistake made during her naive youth, the lord of Hell himself owned her soul which meant that, for the rest of eternity, she would be in his service as a low-level demoness. There was no escape clause—at least, that's what he led her to believe, and up until she thought of throwing herself at the mercy of an angel, she'd definitely believed it.

But before Becca was his, she'd been a devout Catholic who spent the last sixty-six years of her life trying to atone for her fateful mistake. What was done was done. She couldn't go back and change the fact that she gave up her soul for Gabe, but she could make amends for what Lucifer had planned for her after her death.

If there was another thing that she'd learned to believe, it was that anything was possible with the right amount of faith. Back when she was human, she didn't know about the factions and the paranormal beings that ran the night. Only after she was turned into a demoness did she realize there was a whole other world out there.

And one of the factions?

Angels.

For years, she tried to figure out how she could get in contact with one of the celestial beings. Of course, no angel ever visited the Pit, but once Becca was promoted to a temptor—a demon who walked on Earth, in Purgatory, tempting mortals to sin—she had one day out of seven to find one.

And, after wishing and hoping and praying, she had finally managed to, all thanks to a born demoness with a penchant for baking cupcakes.

From the moment she walked past the Twilight

Sweets Bakery, attached to the very same hotel as the bar Becca was currently in, Ariel recognized what Becca was. Instead of showing her prejudices against one of the turned demons, though, she made friends with Becca. And, through Ariel, Becca discovered that the casino in the Twilight Sphere hotel—the aptly named House of Sin—was owned and operated by the three angel princes known as the Angels of Sin City.

Of course, it wasn't as simple as calling them up and asking to meet with them. They were powerful beings, and very busy men. Besides, with Raziel's reputation, she needed to have something worthwhile to trade for what she was really after: her freedom from a contract she signed when she was too young, too lovesick, too *stupid* to know better.

And, after trying to come up with something, anything that he would accept, Becca was hopeful that she finally found it.

Reaching down to the rosary beads she habitually wore wrapped around her wrist, she rubbed the polished beads and prayed again.

She was still praying when, suddenly, she felt like all of the air had been sucked out of the crowded bar.

Or maybe it was just out of her lungs as she gasped.

Because the imposing man that had just walked through the door? She knew without knowing how exactly that that was Raziel, the angel she'd come to meet.

He didn't have his wings out. There was no sign of a burnished halo over his tousled, dark blond curls. But that face? That sharp, chiseled face that was so strikingly beautiful it belonged on a statue… it had 'angel' written all over it.

And, suddenly, Becca wasn't so sure this was a good idea after all.

His steely blue eyes roved over the tables before unerringly settling on hers. He was wearing an expensively tailored business suit—black, so it fit in amongst the bar's decor—and he shook out the perfectly cut jacket before flicking his sleeve, then making his way toward her.

Just as he got to the side of Becca's table, a tall, fit werewolf with a sharp jaw, brown hair, and vibrant green eyes suddenly intercepted Raziel. He clapped him on the shoulders as if they were old friends, and maybe they were. Something told Becca that only a kinship with the other being kept the angel from using his celestial aura against the werewolf for laying his paw on him.

"Hey, there. How are you, buddy? Wasn't expecting you to stop by my fine establishment tonight. Can I get you anything? A drink? Whiskey neat, yeah?"

His gaze flickered over the glass of water and the untouched basket of bread set in the middle of the table. Pursing his lips, Raziel shook his head. "That won't be necessary, Zev. I won't be here long."

Becca swallowed the lump lodged in her throat.

Yup. That didn't bode well at all.

The big werewolf shrugged his shoulders. "No problem. You need me, just shout."

"I will."

With a nod over at Becca, Zev loped away. She watched him murmur something to the waitress who'd been serving her. She immediately turned to avoid their table.

Wonderful. She was really on her own with an angel.

Why hadn't she thought to order a drink that was a little stronger than tap water?

"Um. Hi. You can take a seat if you want."

Raziel raised his eyebrows at her. "No need. I was told you had something to discuss with me. I promised Ariel I could spare five minutes." Glancing down at his watch, he said, "That starts now. Go."

"Sure. Okay. You see, it's about Lucifer's curse."

He was still watching his Rolex. "Gotta be more specific, sweetheart. Lucifer is always cursing the factions. It's what he does."

He didn't understand, did he? If so, he wouldn't be brushing her off like this.

A hint of fury rose over her nerves. "Maybe, but this time he used the fires of Hell to make it really stick."

"Oh?"

Look at that. He finally glanced at her instead of his pricey timepiece.

Becca nodded. "Forged in twilight, he used dark magic to steal the factions' powers for himself."

"Really."

"Yes. From what I heard, it worked, too. But it wasn't just the factions he was aiming for. At least, not in general."

"Why not? He's done it before."

Why not? Good question. The little bit she overhead while working in the Pit didn't quite explain his motivations, but Becca was still sure she was right. "It's not about making other beings' lives hell. It's about destroying the factions entirely. His curse... he targeted it very specifically."

Raziel's eyes seemed to darken. "You're one of his. Why are you telling me this?"

Because she didn't *want* to be Lucifer's.

"Because it's not right. And because, if you don't already know, you should."

"And why's that?" A quick peek at his wrist. "Three minutes."

Becca tried not to get too flustered. What was the worst that could happen?

Well, Lucifer could find out she was telling one of his mortal enemies secrets that she overhead in his domain, hoping to using it against him...

Becca squeezed the onyx bead on her rosary,

grateful for the familiar chill of the stone. "He went for the heart of each one," she blurted out. "He's cursed all of you. The royals of each faction."

"All of us?" To her surprise, Raziel pulled back one of the stools, climbing on top of it as he faced Becca. Obviously, she'd caught his interest at last. "What do you mean, *all* of us?"

Becca swallowed. "Angels, too. He's cursed you and the other princes."

Raziel didn't say anything for a moment. He just watched her with those dark blue eyes, as if he could see right through her.

Could he? He was an angel, a powerful one to be considered a prince among his kind, and even if he'd been living on the mortal plane for longer than Becca wanted to imagine, his powerful aura was a crackle against her overheated skin.

And then he lifted his hand, catching the attention of the oversized werewolf still looming nearby.

"Zev? I think I'll take that drink after all."

WAS SHE LYING?

Demons lie. It was what they did. Whether they were born into the faction like most of their kind, or turned like some others—the demons came to mind, as did the vampires—demons had a few defining characteristics.

They lied. They cheated. They tricked. If the devil's in the details, then the trap lies with his henchman. Lucifer might have been the most infamous of Raze's kind once upon a time, but he'd become something different in the millennia since. Something evil. Chaotic.

Cruel.

The lord of the demons, and an enemy of most of the factions—including Raze and his brothers.

There was definitely no love lost between the former fallen angel and the Angels of Sin City. Though they were all kicked out of Heaven ages ago, Lucifer relished his new role as the lord of Hell. He didn't understand why Raze, Sam, and Micah were so desperate to find their way back home, and if Raze suspected that Lucifer had something to do with their missing talisman, he kept it to himself.

Raze ruled his corner of the City of Sin. The humans he was forced to interact with thought of him as a god; truth be told, they weren't too far off. He controlled House of Sin, making money, making deals, making plans. But even if he was the most powerful angel in Las Vegas—a fact his two brothers would undoubtedly agree with—he wasn't strong enough to take on Lucifer.

And, honestly? He didn't really want to. Whatever

Lucifer was up to, so long as he didn't interfere with Raze and his brothers, Raze couldn't care less.

Until now.

Until he reluctantly agreed to meet with a woman and he found *her*.

With her angelic features, her wary grey eyes, and the rosary she wore like a bracelet 'round her slender wrist, she was nothing like the demons he'd faced off against—but no matter how weak his senses were these days, Raze was sure of it: she was a demoness, and she was risking *everything* by coming to him.

Zev returned with two glasses in hand—well, *paw*. A whiskey neat for Raze that he sat in front of him, and a fresh glass of lemon water that he placed next to the female's barely drunk first one.

Raze drew his glass closer to him. "Thanks."

"Don't mention it, Raze."

"Raze." Her brow furrowed as Zev went to talk to the bears at the next table. "I thought your name was Raziel."

After taking a sip of his drink, Raze nodded. "It is."

"Oh. Um. I'm Rebecca, by the way. Becca, really. No one ever calls me Rebecca."

She was still nervous. Raze felt her anxiety like needles pricking his skin.

Another sip, then he drawled, "What do you know about angels?"

She toyed with the straw from her first glass, not

quite meeting his eyes. Fidgety female. "Angels in general," she asked, "or the Angels of Sin City?"

Ah. So she'd heard about him and his brothers. He'd expected as such; all of the local factions knew about them. He'd wondered when Ariel insisted that he be the one to meet with her friend if it was because he was one of the Angels of Sin City—considered a prince among their kind due to their (formerly) potent celestial auras and how long they'd managed to survive in Purgatory—or because he was the wealthy owner of the House of Sin casino.

For millennia, it was his wings and his aura and his angelic senses that made Raze untouchable. This last century, things shifted. He couldn't remember the last time he spread his wings and took a flight just for pleasure and not for business. So consumed with running the casino, it had been easy to fall into the guise of a powerful *mortal* businessman more often than not.

The fact that the three angel princes' powers had been noticeably waning over the last few years made it easier to pretend. It didn't do a damn thing for the homesickness, or Raze's stubborn determination that he'd bring his brothers back to Heaven one day, but his dulled senses had him at least questioning the undeniable way he was drawn to the redheaded demoness.

"Forget about that." Telling her about soulmates and what it meant to be bonded to an angel could wait —and not just the minute and a half left from her initial five. It had been a dick move to hold her to it, mainly because he was still stunned at his realization, but now things were... different. "You mentioned a curse."

She nodded. A strand of her wavy red hair fluttered over her shoulder, curling against the pale skin of her cleavage.

The sudden desire to brush it away had Raze fisting his hand. He wasn't sure which was the bigger temptation: to see how silky soft her hair was or how nice her skin would feel against his fingertips.

Forcing his hand open, Raze flexed his fingers before reaching for his glass. Tilting his head back, he swallowed the last of his drink. He relished the slight burn, then narrowed his gaze on her.

"I won't insult either of us by pretending that my senses haven't confirmed you're being honest with me. Obviously, there's another curse. Lucifer's fucking with the rest of us again. Now, tell me how you know about it."

Becca bit her bottom lip, and the cynical male that Raze had grown into over the centuries wondered if it was a calculated gesture. Was she trying to entice him? If so, she'd have an easy job of it. From the moment Raze walked into the Twilight Bar and Grille, he'd been drawn to her. The longer he sat across from her, the harder it was to ignore.

God, he needed another drink.

CHAPTER 3

To make matters worse, the slight nibble had Raze's body going even tighter.

No doubt about that. Decades of celibacy would do that to any male, he'd bet, but it was the unfamiliar ache in his chest that had his scowl deepening.

She was nervous. More than that, she was *afraid*.

And that, he decided, was unacceptable.

He swallowed, deciding on the right sort of tone, before gentling his clipped voice until he sounded like he was asking her to explain rather than demanding as he said, "If this affects my brothers and me, I should know. Let's start from the beginning. Where did you hear this?"

Becca tucked the stray strand of flame-red hair behind her ear. He mourned the missed opportunity, then tightened his jaw before the expression flashed across his face.

"Dane." His blank expression must've given away his ignorance because she quickly added, "A werewolf. He was there when the curse was made and has been telling any being he can about it for ages now. I mean, I'm a demon and even *I* heard that Lucifer's turned his attention to the royals. Didn't you?"

No. Raze had not.

But he should have.

The royals... She didn't mean just Raze and his brothers. While Lucifer's curse would have probably targeted them regardless—and that definitely explained their waning powers—if he was taking on all of the royals, he had his hands full.

It was how the factions were designed. While the community itself was considered paranormal, each individual group was arranged around what *type* of being you were. There were angels and demons, the celestial races. Shifters, including werewolves, bears, and the rarer phoenixes. Witches. Vampires. Even fairies.

And every faction was ruled by a family that, for all intents and purposes, was considered "royal". There were no kings, not really. No queens, either. The factions weren't a monarchy like the humans understood, but a few leaders who were more powerful than the rest of the beings who earned the title.

In their world, might made right. The strong led. Everyone else followed.

But what happened when the strength was gone?

For longer than he wanted to admit, their power had been disappearing. Micah confessed he felt it, too; if pressed, so did Sam. Their angelic senses were fading, the last of their lingering connection to the celestial cities in Heaven weakening, and if he noticed that he was shedding feathers on the rare occasion he went for a midnight flight over Las Vegas, Raze was stubborn enough to ignore the trail of black feathers he left behind him.

It made sense if they were cursed. In fact, it explained a lot.

What it didn't explain, though?

Was this meeting.

"Why are you telling me?" he asked. "The demoness who arranged for me to meet with you—"

"Ariel," Becca supplied.

"Right. She insisted that I be the one to come down to the bar to talk to you. Why me?"

Did she know? An angel was blessed to recognize his or her soulmate on sight. Was it the same for demons?

Though he didn't really pay too much attention to the other factions—too busy with his brothers and their business to really care, to be honest—he thought that pure demons were the same as angels in that way.

Turned demons—humans who sold their soul to Lucifer—wouldn't know, but if she'd been born into the faction...

She swallowed roughly. He watched the slight movement of her slender, pale throat and forced himself to stifle the groan he felt rising in his.

"Because I need your help," she said at last.

Damn it. Where the fuck was Zev? Or any other server? He wanted that refill *yesterday.*

It took a moment before he realized that she had answered him. When he did, he raised his eyebrows. "Me? In particular?"

"Yes."

Did she know?

"Why?"

"Because you're an angel. Ariel said you were the most powerful one. To me, that means that, of all the factions, you're the only one who can take on Lucifer. I'll give you this"—digging her hand in the front pocket of her jeans, Becca pulled out a folded sheet of paper—"if you'll agree to protect me against him."

Honestly, he would've immediately agreed to do it if only because his instincts were begging him to grab her, to touch her, to kiss her, to *claim* her. Soothing her worry and her fear was another bonus; he was a fallen angel, but even if he had a long-standing distaste for the other factions, he hated to see another soul in pain.

Especially if she was his soulmate.

It didn't even matter what was on that sheet, though when Becca admitted it was the exact wording of the curse as best as she'd been able to pin down, he found himself eager to grab it.

But he didn't. Instead, he leaned back in his seat and asked, "And why exactly would I need to protect you?"

It was a valid question. And from the way the little color left in her face drained away, Raze almost regretted asking it.

Almost.

If this was a set-up, he needed to know what he was getting into. A curse was one thing. Welcoming a demoness into his casino, especially one who was looking for protection from Lucifer... he had to ask.

And no, it had nothing to do with an intense desire to learn everything about Becca, why do you ask?

She shuddered out a breath. "Because Lucifer owns my soul. I left the Pit and I don't want to go back, but if he discovers that I'm staying up here, he'll come after me. And," she added, daring a glimpse up at Raze's gruff expression, "if he knows that I gave you a copy of the curse, he'll make me pay for betraying him."

Forget the drink. Raze needed to be stone-cold sober to finish the rest of this conversation.

Becca was his soulmate. He knew it to the depths of his being. What the fuck did she mean that *Lucifer* owned hers?

"How the hell did he get his hands on your soul?"

She flinched, turning away. Despite being so very pale, twin spots of pink rose high on her cheeks. Nervousness became shame as she admitted, "I was young. Stupid. I fell in love"—oof, not what he wanted to hear when he was fighting the instinct to run away with her only minutes after he first laid eyes on her— "with the wrong man. He promised me anything if only I'd give him *everything*. I did. I sold my soul for that man only to have him disappear on me. That was, oh, so many years ago, but I've sworn all other men off completely ever since. Especially after my time in the Pit and... and, Jesus, I don't know why I'm telling you all of this."

Raze did. Because Becca instinctively recognized Raze, too, even if she couldn't quite understand why. Lucifer might have tricked her into signing away her soul and making her one of his demons, but that only meant he did Raze a favor. Instead of being a mortal who lived, then died before he ever met her, Becca was an immortal demoness who'd found a way to break free of the Pit—the demons' name for their corner of Hell—if only long enough to have this meeting.

She was right, though. Even if she wasn't his soul-mate, Raze's celestial aura—coupled with his brothers and the angels he employed at the casino—was at least enough to shield her for as long as she wanted to hide from Lucifer.

Of course, that meant she needed to be near him for his aura to cover hers. A room in the Twilight Sphere hotel—the huge, faction-run hotel that housed all of the Twilight properties including this bar and Raze's casino—for a start, and maybe a job. He could hide her in plain sight, give her something to do, and then retreat to his office where he could put some distance between them.

He'd protect her. For so many reasons—and, okay, one of them had everything to do with the paper clutched tightly between her slender fingers and the faint hope that it might be the answer to his weakening powers—he'd protect her.

But claim her?

Admit to her—or any other soul—that she was his soulmate?

Make a move on a female who was obviously afraid, on the run, and who just said earnestly that she'd sworn off all males?

No. He couldn't.

So he wouldn't.

"What did you do for Lucifer?"

Her eyes skittered back to him. She looked surprised that Raze didn't comment on her confession, but she was quick to follow his lead and change the subject.

And if he also experienced the hope welling up in her, Raze stoically pretended that he couldn't.

"I'm a low-level demon. For six out of seven days, I spend sixteen hours at my desk, assigning souls to their torment. On the seventh, I'm allowed to come back to Purgatory and try to tempt men to sin. Not the best job, I know, but I had a quota. If I didn't meet it..." She dropped her gaze to her lap, the fingers on her right hand running over the rosary beads wrapped around her left. Raze got the idea that it was a reflexive gesture, one that Becca did out of habit. "Anyway, that's how I was able to come here today. If I'm not back in the Pit by sun-up, Lucifer will know I've gone rogue."

Tempt men to sin... she was doing a number on him right now, for sure. And, from the waves of lust coming from many of the other patrons in the bar, he wasn't the only one. Becca was the perfect package: she had the beauty, the innocent edge, and the sultry pout that men would gladly sell their souls to kiss—or more.

"If you know anything about me, you know that I own House of Sin. I'm also not a true angel, but one of the Fallen. Tempting sinners is practically the family business. You'd fit in well there, Becca."

Her eyes widened. It had the effect of making her even more alluring, a fact that Raze was sure she was completely oblivious to. "Are you offering me a job at your casino?"

"It's the best way to shield you. There are rules here. In the hotel... in the casino, you'd be safe."

"And I can earn my own way if you'd let me. That's all I want," she said, her voice dropping to a murmur. "I just want a second chance."

Wasn't that what most beings wanted?

"I can always use more servers. Can you take an order? A drink order?"

"Um. Yeah. I'm sure I can."

"Then you're hired."

"And you'll protect me from Lucifer?" Becca asked.

Raze tapped his pointer finger against the tabletop before gesturing to the scrap of paper she was still holding onto. "Toss that my way and we've got a deal."

A giddy laugh escaped his pretty soulmate as she slid it toward him. "Gladly."

CHAPTER 4

He thought some distance would help.

It *didn't*.

When he could finally bring himself to leave her, Raze gave Becca his card with his personal cell number, told her to head to the casino that night at eight o'clock sharp, then made his escape. With every forceful step of his dress shoe, he hoped that the tugging would quit. That he would outpace the urge to turn around and blurt out, "Come home with me," to the demoness.

He wasn't sure if he should blame Lucifer or God almighty just then for the turn in his fortune. Raze had managed to avoid chancing on his soulmate for ages only to discover her in a human-turned-demoness who spent the last few years working for his enemy. Not only that, but how could he admit the truth to her right after she told him about a curse that could only be broken once Raze found his true mate?

Because that's what the lines on the page meant. Between the rumors spread by the werewolf who'd been lucky—or, perhaps, *un*lucky enough to spy on Lucifer during his casting of the curse—and Becca keeping her ear cocked in Hell, she was certain that she had the curse captured on paper.

The curse was straight forward enough. She was right when she told Raze that Lucifer targeted the heads of each faction, the royals.

Sever them in three...

Each faction was ruled by three royals; some princes, some princesses.

The nearest object the curse will keep...

Just like how the angel princes imprinted on their key to Heaven, the other factions had a sacred talisman that served as the cornerstone of their power. The cursed object? It had to be, Raze decided.

One to true love it will be...

And that was the part that had Raze fighting against the pull toward Becca. For an angel, a true love could only be one person: his soulmate.

Who—surprise, surprise—was Rebecca Murphy, a demoness who was willing to beg for his help to avoid Raze's old enemy. Raze, however, had been in the casino business long enough to know a bad bet when he saw one in front of him.

He could save her, but he couldn't have her; just because fate wanted to interfere with the life he worked so hard to achieve, that didn't mean he had to go along with it. So, rather than prolong their meeting at the Twilight Bar and Grille, he flagged down Zev again, told him to put everything Becca ordered on his tab, then made his curt goodbyes.

He made sure to tell her that he was a busy angel, and that she would be reporting to Cael. His floor manager would get her set up with a job and a rented room, but if she needed anything—*anything*—at all, she was free to call him.

That whole first night, he willed his damn phone to ring.

It didn't. And, considering Cael was a trusted angel, once Raze told him to take good care of the new demoness hire, he honestly didn't expect there to be any problems. As the floor manager, Cael had full control over the day-to-day workings of the casino, from the security team to the maintenance crew, as well as the serving team.

To get patrons to feed more bills into the slots, House of Sin offered an assortment of free beverages all served by strikingly beautiful male and female servers. Becca, he knew, was enticing enough that she would no doubt rake in the tips. A win-win for them all. She'd be flush with cash while the casino would benefit from such a stunning addition to the staff.

And Raze spent hours trying to convince himself of that.

Yeah. It didn't work.

Micah noticed, too. While Sam was still conveniently missing, Micah was in the office when Raze came storming back to the casino after meeting with Becca. Even more gruff and short-tempered than he'd been before he left, he snapped at Micah when his youngest brother asked how the mysterious meeting went. He didn't say a damn thing other than Lucifer was back to being a major asshole, that the rumors of the curse were true, and they had a new hire.

From the puzzled look on Micah's face as he turned around and left the office again, Raze guessed his brother was having a hard time figuring what one thing had to do with another. A new hire wasn't unusual, even if Raze rarely paid attention to staffing issues; that was usually Sam's department. Being cursed by Lucifer? Sadly, that was nothing new, either.

Raze in a pissy mood?

Nope. That, at least, was strictly normal.

Raze leaving work early and locking himself in his executive suite on the top floor of the hotel?

That... that was new. And when Micah risked paging him later that night, Raze covered it up by explaining that he'd left the Bar and Grille on the main floor with a pounding headache and, for once, he was turning in early.

It wasn't really a lie. Raze's skull was pounding, his brain beating against the inside of it, so headache? Oh, yeah. He had to admit that it was still stretching the truth a little since it wasn't the headache that had him confined to his quarters, pacing his oversized bedroom back and forth.

It was the bond.

The invisible tether that burst into existence the moment he looked into Becca's grey eyes, and that kept yanking on him, demanding that he return to the casino level where—at that very moment—Becca was starting her first shift under Cael's watchful gaze.

Once he locked himself inside of his suite, Raze turned to the well-stocked bar he kept. He'd never really considered himself much of a drinker—he made it through all of Prohibition without a single sip, after all, if only because Sam took a liking to one of the teetotalers—but a whiskey here or there never hurt. Down at the bar, he'd only had the one drink. Up in his suite? He finished off the bottle, his celestial metabolism burning through the alcohol before he really got a good buzz going.

And, still, he had to fight the instinct to return to her.

That was ridiculous, right? A female he had spoken to for maybe twenty minutes tops—well past his initial five—she shouldn't have this much control over him? He was an angel, for God's sake. Even if Lucifer's blasted curse had stolen his powers bit by bit, he should be the one calling her to him, not the other way around.

One of an angel's less revealed abilities was the power of suggestion. He couldn't quite make a lesser being do what he wanted them to do without any consequence, but if Raze or one of his brothers put some effort into it, there were few who could resist falling under his sway. Lore said that it wouldn't work on a soulmate, though Raze wasn't willing to test that theory. He was trying to avoid Becca, not use his power to make her fall for him.

Even if, he admitted the next morning, he was already lost.

Raze blamed it on the bond. He'd heard it was a powerful thing, that stronger males than him had tried —and *failed*—to fight it. Soulmates, especially when it came to the angelic faction, were basically inevitable.

And he told himself *that* once he made the reckless decision to check on Becca in time for her second shift that night.

In the end, the stubborn angel gave himself credit for waiting a whole twenty-four hours. It was enough time for Becca to settle in, to learn her duties, to have spent a night—*it better have been alone*, grumbled Raze —in the room Cael set up for her on the thirteenth floor of the hotel. As her new boss, it was only fair that he saw that she was getting on okay.

And if this was the first time ever that he interfered with one of the staff, Raze refused to acknowledge it. Because while Becca was now an employee of House of Sin, she was also his soulmate and Raze couldn't deny that no matter how hard he tried.

Just so it wasn't *that* obvious, Raze sought out Cael first. The moment he stepped onto the casino floor, he felt the yank leading him to the north side and instinctively knew that that was where he would find Becca. Purposely turning his back on it, he flagged down his floor manager instead, making small talk about the evening's events before he just... just couldn't stand it any longer.

Clapping Cael on the back, telling him to keep up the good work, he left a visibly stunned angel behind as he intently marched to where Becca had just finished dropping off a pair of cocktails to a married pair nickel-and-diming a neighboring set of slots.

She accepted the singles they passed her way, a beaming smile lighting up her face. Raze nearly missed a step when he caught the quirk of her lips even from her side profile.

Or maybe that was the outfit she was wearing.

Oh, Lord, help me.

As if she could sense his approach—or his sudden arousal as his body immediately reacted to her presence—Becca turned. To his surprise, she blinked, momentarily stunned, before her smile actually widened.

For him, Raze thought in a daze. She was smiling at him.

Too bad it didn't last.

"Hi— uh." Her smile faltered. "Is something wrong?"

Shit. Was he drooling? He was definitely fucking staring, and he corrected that by quickly blinking. With a swipe of the back of his hand against his chin, he was relieved to see that he'd managed to keep his saliva inside of his mouth, before he smoothly ran his fingers through his styled hair.

Raze shook his head, trying to keep his composure. It was one thing to see Becca with her hair loose, her body covered, her face free of make-up. But this? Between the expertly applied lipstick and eyeliner, the short skirt and cropped top, and her beautiful red hair curled up and clipped out of her gorgeous face?

Oh, yeah. It was a near miss that he *wasn't* drooling.

The server's uniform was revealing on purpose. The males went around shirtless, while the females left their legs and their shoulders on display. It was a distraction for the patrons as well as a way for the servers to use any advantage for their tips. Anyone uncomfortable with the cut could wear something that covered more of their skin, but very few did.

He wasn't sure if he was happy or pissed that Becca went along with the same uniform.

It was her choice, he reminded himself. Even if she was his soulmate, he could never control her. What she did, what she wore... that was up to Becca.

But, hell, he wished she'd keep that delicious little body hidden to everyone except for him.

And that tattoo...

Vaguely, he remembered the way she wore a rosary around her wrist. Glancing down if only for a second, Raze noticed it was still there. An odd accessory for a demoness, but even odder when he reveled in the elaborate design on her skin.

Roses. From the top of her shoulder, down to the crook of her elbow, covering her arm, her side, and part of her back, Becca was covered in deep-red roses mingled with thorny vines and—holy shit—was that a cross nestled in there?

Rosary... what was another name for a rosary but a wreath of roses? And she wore it proudly on her left side, near her heart.

Huh. Perhaps the rosary wasn't just an accessory after all.

CHAPTER 5

Becca followed the direction of Raze's open stare and, immediately, got the wrong idea.

"Oh." She slid her hand over her chest, covering as much of her tattoo with her hand. "Is this okay? I didn't think... I know that, when I was still human, a lot of places didn't like visible tattoos. But with this outfit—"

Raze still eyed the deep-red petals peeking through her slender fingers. "It's fine."

It wasn't fine, but not for the reason Becca obviously thought.

This... this was unusual. This bubbling jealousy that would've turned his blue eyes green if it were possible. He had no idea she was hiding such a work of art etched into her skin, but now that he knew? He wanted to explore every line, every detail of the ink. He wanted to worship it—worship *her*—but, like mood-changing eyes for angels, it just wasn't possible.

She might be his soulmate, but he was her boss. More than that, he was supposed to be protecting her from Lucifer and his sycophants. Leering at Becca was inappropriate in so many ways, least of all because she didn't seem to know what to make of it.

The last thing he wanted was for her to think she was doing something wrong. Beneath her angelic smile and her innocent demeanor, his senses recognized a guarded soul that was both wounded and hardened after her years working for Lucifer. It took everything she had to break free from his clutches, and Raze was grateful that she had.

True, he couldn't shake the suspicion that she was a plant, that Lucifer had pushed her toward Raze on purpose. If he knew that the demoness was Raze's soulmate, he had no doubt that his old enemy would get a kick out of using Becca as a tempting lure for the one soul who could never resist her.

But he would have to.

Even if Becca wasn't a trap set by Lucifer, he couldn't just drop the bomb on her that she was his fated mate. As a former human, she wouldn't recognize him for what he was, and she already made it clear that she didn't believe in the concept of soulmates. Why would she when believing in the "one" was what landed her in the Pit in the first place? She didn't turn to Raze because she wanted a lover. She wanted a protector—and she would get one.

It wasn't just the jealousy that was making his teeth grind. It was the possessive urge to watch over her, to make sure she was safe. They'd known each other for barely two days, but that didn't matter to Raze. In a way, it was as if he'd *always* known Becca. As soon as he felt the pull toward her, as soon as he knew unmistakably that she was meant for him alone, it was like he'd been waiting for her all along.

Was that what it was like to find his lifemate? He wasn't a shifter. While the factions were full of all sorts of predatory animals masquerading as men and women, Raze was a royal angel. He expected, if he actually stumbled on his soul's mate, that it wouldn't change him.

A day and a half after he walked into the Twilight Bar and Grille and already Raze admitted that he'd been full of shit.

And, worse, he'd put the most tempting female he'd ever met before in his long, long life right where he could never touch her: in his employ.

God, *damn* it.

———

ANOTHER NIGHT, ANOTHER SHIFT, AND BECCA COULDN'T shake the feeling that she was being watched.

It was a sixth sense she honed during her time in the Pit. Though her level of demon was akin to a pencil-pusher in a cramped office full of never-ending cubicles, she never once forgot who she worked for. And her bosses? They really *were* from Hell.

She'd never forget poor Simon, either. He'd had the cubicle across from hers. Cream of the crop, star of their immediate office, and he accidentally asked for a meager water break during their sixteen-hour shift when the floor lead was in a foul mood. Jerroz pointed a black talon at Simon and engulfed him in flames. Only then, when he was almost entirely burned to a crisp, did Jerroz toss a half-empty glass of stagnant water on Simon.

His screams were etched into Becca's memory, even now. The stench of flesh on fire and burning hair took months to leave her nostrils, and the black patch of what used to be Simon was a constant reminder even after Peter took over the cubicle.

She'd seen a lot during her service to Lucifer. But that? That had given her the push she needed to find some way to break out of the Pit.

Then, when she added the rumors swirling around Sin City and added it to the few snippets she picked up while she was working, she hoped—she *prayed*—that she would find sanctuary with Raziel.

With *Raze*.

Becca flushed at just the thought of him.

It had barely been a week since she did the bravest —though not reckless, since that title definitely belonged to the impulsive way she sold her soul to Lucifer—thing she'd ever done in her life: throw herself at the mercy of the cold, calculating angel prince.

Only Raze was nothing like the image of barely restrained fury and ice that she'd been led to expect. Sure, he'd seemed that way when he first entered the bar, but it wasn't long before Becca understood that there was more to the imposing angel than she initially thought.

Cold? Hardly. There was untapped fire deep inside of that stunning male, and Becca was a demoness straight from Hell. If anyone knew about flames, it was her.

Fury? Maybe. She'd caught a few glimpses of a leashed anger in the time since she'd known him, but not at her. Never at her. So while Becca was positive that he wasn't a man she wanted to get on the wrong side of, he didn't frighten her. Not anymore.

In fact, she found herself looking forward to his inevitable visits while she was making the rounds on the casino floor. No matter how busy he was—and she knew that Raze had to have plenty of demands on his time—he always tracked her down, if only for a few minutes' chat, leaving her almost breathless when he left again.

Sometimes, she had to resist the impulse to place down her tray and follow after him. It was almost a compulsion, and one she struggled to ignore.

It would be so much easier if he didn't look at her the way he did. As if she was a woman, and not a lowly demon. As if she deserved to be under his protection rather than just a means to an end for the infamously shrewd businessman.

In the days since she started as a server, she'd gotten used to being watched. It was usually harmless, though. The patrons who ogled her the most tended to be the biggest tippers so she didn't really mind. She'd been able to dodge any of their advances, each one taking her rejection pretty well.

Of course, when the casino's security team was made up of bulky, powerful werewolves, the patrons—whether they were faction or human—tended to be pretty well-mannered. And that wasn't even taking into account the owners' reputations.

She felt safe in the casino. Safer than she had in longer than she could remember. The pay, so far, was good, the patrons generous, and she'd only been there for a week. There'd been no sign of Lucifer or any of his henchmen; in fact, she was the only human-turned-demon in the casino as far as she could tell, if not the whole hotel. It seemed as if Raze knew what he was doing when he said he could protect her from Lucifer.

Now, if only she could protect her heart from *him*.

As she passed her by, Candi nudged Becca in the side. She fought the urge to wince; her fellow server was a fairy and, while delicate, she had the *pointiest* elbow. Instead, she glanced over at her.

Cocking her empty tray against her hip while using her equally pointed chin, Candi gestured beyond the poker tables.

Becca looked.

Well. That would explain it.

Raze was standing there, lurking in the shadows just out of reach of the glitz and glamour and neon lights of the casino. Every now and then, the lights would flare, throwing his beautiful features into relief, while he leaned against the wall at his back. He had his legs braced, his arms crossed over his broad chest.

And he was watching her.

As she met his stare, he didn't move. Honestly, she wasn't even sure he blinked.

Becca waved.

He nodded, but stayed in the shadows.

Candi was the first of the servers to introduce herself to Becca. They shared the same shifts, and Cael —the floor manager for the whole casino—left Candi to train Becca her first night. They'd become fast friends since then, even if Candi found it adorable that Becca had one of the big bosses looking out for her.

Without going into details why, she tried to explain

that Raze just wanted to make sure she was adjusting to the job all right. Candi patted her sweetly on the shoulder before joking that she hoped Becca remembered the little people when Raze finally pounced.

Since she didn't think that would happen, Becca just shrugged Candi's teasing off.

In exchange for the information on Lucifer's curse, he was watching out for her. That was all.

And she managed to convince herself of that until one of the werewolf security members joined Candi and Becca near the edge of the casino floor.

Though he was nowhere near as beautiful as Raze, Anthony was ruggedly handsome in a wolfish sort of way. With his shaggy, dirty blond hair and bright gold eyes, he was as sinful as most other beings in this city. And, since the first night Becca worked the floor, he'd been finding reasons to stop her and chat.

He'd already asked her to dinner twice before. Because he seemed like a nice guy, Becca kept pushing him off. He tried to lay it out like she was new to the Twilight scene and he was just interested in giving her a tour, but then she caught his shifter's gaze roving over her body and she knew exactly what he was interested in touring—and it wasn't the hotel.

She settled on a maybe, if only because it might be nice to go out to dinner with someone else eventually. Each time she did, he took the rejection graciously, though that didn't stop him from asking again anyway.

After the three of them made small talk for a few seconds—all they could really spare without Cael getting on their ass—Becca was expecting Anthony to ask her what time she was getting off shift when, instead, he chuckled under his breath.

"Uh oh," Anthony said jovially. "Incoming."

Candi immediately lifted her tray. "On that note, I'm out. Sorry, guys. I need this job too much to piss off one of the princes."

One of the—

Becca spun around.

Gliding through the crowd, moving like a shark who had an unblinking gaze locked on its prey, she found him.

Raze.

And *she* was his target.

CHAPTER 6

She looked surprised at his sudden appearance.

To be honest, so was Raze.

He'd been finding too many reasons to distract Becca while she was working which, in turn, was becoming a huge distraction for Raze.

Yeah. His whole "stay away from my soulmate" plan had barely lasted a night. But he was trying. It wasn't going so great, but he *was* trying. With Sam still MIA and Micah doing... whatever he was doing, he'd managed to avoid his brothers figuring out that their new hire was anything other than a pretty face to work the crowds and get the patrons to spend more money. Becca seemed happy at the casino, and a few pointed questions to the hotel team confirmed that she went to bed alone every night.

It was the most he could hope for—until Cael let slip that Anthony, in security, had been paying close attention to the new demoness.

He should let other males woo Becca. If he couldn't bring himself to claim her as his soulmate, there was no reason she shouldn't be able to pick a different lover. Just because he was a stubborn old fool, that didn't mean she should be punished.

He couldn't have her—but as he watched Anthony sidle up to Becca from across the casino, Raze couldn't remember a single reason *why* he was fighting this.

Most beings had a fated mate out there. It was part of the magic that made them different from mortals. On top of each individual faction's powers, skill, and abilities, they could create a lifebond with a predetermined mate.

Raze had never searched for his before. He had been too busy surviving as one of the Fallen, taking care of his brothers, and looking for a return to Heaven to worry about finding the other half of his soul.

After falling to Purgatory, he cycled through the seven deadly sins. Raze was able to shake off some of them quite easily: envy, sloth, gluttony. Wrath was harder to control in the beginning, though that faded as Raze grew harder. Colder. More determined to succeed. However, pride was one he could never shake, and greed kept him always working for more.

Then there was lust.

Of course, like most males, he had needs. As soon as he had a few gold coins to spare, he'd find the best companions in the most respectable brothels as he could. One night every few decades was enough, though the time between matings grew longer as pride took root in his soul.

He wanted wealth. He wanted power. He wanted to never want for anything, and as the centuries passed him by, he found more pleasure in a business deal than in a paid-for pussy.

Raze and his brothers went from shepherds to farmers to kings. The royal angels of Sin City. Gone were the days where he had to pay for sex. For centuries, women chased Raze—and he took his pick on the rare occasion he wanted to have someone else worship his cock. He didn't have to resort to prostitutes any longer, but Raze made no mistake in believing that it was anything more than a physical act. In fact, he paid his modern companions far more for a few fucks than the gold coins he kept in a pouch at his side for those midnight trips to the local brothels.

But after what happened to Micah four decades ago—when he loved, then lost his soulmate before he could claim her—Raze realized that he never wanted to be responsible for a soulmate of his own. She would be a weakness he couldn't afford, especially now that he knew the reality of Lucifer's curse.

That, at least, he had shared with Micah. He didn't

tell his brother where he'd gotten the page with Becca's delicate scrawl written on it, and Micah pointedly didn't ask. When the lines made it perfectly clear that the curse wouldn't be broken unless the brothers found both their missing talisman and claimed their soulmates, it didn't really matter.

Micah lost his.

Raze stubbornly refused to approach Becca.

And Sam...

Well. He was Sam.

They were fucked. The curse would only continue to steal their power, and what happened when the other angels found out? They'd been the princes for centuries, but that didn't mean there weren't other beings looking to usurp their throne.

Becca knew what the curse said. She had to, since she gave it to him. Now that it became clear he would need to bond her to him to break the curse, he *definitely* couldn't claim her. No doubt she would figure that he was only paying her attention because he needed her, not that he cared.

But he did. Damn it, it had barely been a week, and he cared so fucking much he almost wanted to tear his heart from his chest for just a moment's relief.

Was this what it was like to be in love? With a fated mate, the bond was instant. Lust, too. Love was usually an afterthought, but everything he learned about Becca since they met, every time she flashed him a shaky smile that grew more confident with the next... Raze knew lust. He knew attraction. He knew what it was like to need to fuck so bad, his balls were turning blue.

This was different.

For the first time ever, his heart was involved.

And he fucking *hated* it.

If it was just lust, he could've seduced her. Tempting a demoness had a bit of irony a fallen angel would appreciate, and he was sure he'd more than enjoy Becca's body. But it wasn't just lust. She was his soulmate, the one female fated to be his, and because his heart *was* involved, he had to put her first—and putting her first meant leaving her the hell alone.

But when Anthony leaned in, smirking slyly as his golden gaze darted down Becca's already low-cut shirt, Raze realized that he couldn't pretend to be noble any longer.

Hey. He was one of the Fallen for a reason. And this Fallen?

One way or another, he was going to stake his claim.

Striding purposely across the casino, he watched as the perky blonde fairy quickly made her escape. The werewolf, on the other hand, stayed where he was.

Good, thought Raze. As powerful as Anthony was, he wasn't an alpha wolf. In a challenge, Raze would win—and when it came to Becca, he was ready to challenge any potential suitors.

With a quick, careful nod toward Becca, he met the shifter's golden eyes dead-on. "Anthony. Check in with Cael. I'm sure he needs you to make your rounds."

"I already did."

"Do them again."

"Where, boss?"

"Wherever Becca isn't."

Anthony saluted him, a tease in his golden wolf's eyes. "Gotcha, boss."

Raze stayed perched next to Becca, waiting for Anthony to leave. Before the wily werewolf had, though, he tapped her on her shoulder. "Hey, Becca?"

She'd been stealing a glance up at Raze before Anthony called her name. When she turned away to answer, Raze let a snarl rip across his face, knowing she wouldn't see but that Anthony would.

The werewolf ignored Raze completely as Becca said, "Yes?"

"Before I go, I just wanted to see what you were doing tonight. You down for dinner when you get off shift?"

Oh. The werewolf had a death wish, did he?

Damn it. If only he wasn't one of the best of the security team, Raze might unleash his wings, snatch the big werewolf, fly up to the top of the Twilight Sphere, and drop him down to the Strip below.

Anthony would survive, but the time spent regenerating all of his smashed bones should serve as the perfect warning to back off of Becca—

No. That wasn't fair to his soulmate. Even if she wanted to date Anthony, it wasn't fair of him to take his frustrations out on the werewolf if only because he had the balls to ask her out first.

But Becca hadn't said yes. Before she could, Raze found himself answering for her. "Sorry. I'm afraid that won't be possible. Becca's not free tonight."

"Oh. Is that so?"

The furry bastard was pushing him. Too late to realize what Anthony was doing, Raze let him do it.

"Yes. She's having dinner with me."

Becca's head whipped back toward him so quickly, one of her curls escaped its clip. "I am?"

He took her hand, squeezing it gently. "You are."

She blinked, then gave him one of those heart-stopping smiles. "Then I guess I am."

Okay, Raze decided when a self-satisfied smirk tugged on Anthony's lips before he winked over at him.

Maybe he'd give the interloping shifter a fucking raise after all.

———

BECCA VERY NEARLY BACKED OUT OF GOING TO DINNER with Raze.

There were so many reasons why she should kindly turn him down. After Gabe, Becca had decided to never get involved with a man again. And Raze... he wasn't just a man.

He was her boss.

He was her protector.

Hell, he was a freaking *angel*.

And, yet, when Raze offered to take her out to celebrate her freedom at the Twilight Bar and Grille that night, she forgot every single last one of those reasons.

Turned out, when she wasn't pissing herself in fear that he would turn her away and she'd be left at the mercy of Lucifer, sitting down to have a meal with Raze was actually really nice. In fact, the evening was so incredibly enjoyable that when Raze invited her out the next night, she said 'yes" again before she even thought about it.

Besides, it wasn't like his unexpected interest in her would last, right?

Wrong.

That first dinner was just the beginning. At the end of every shift—whether it was six in the evening, four in the morning, or noon—Raze was there to take her to dinner. Eventually, dinner turned into breakfasts when he was free, and exploring the whole of the Twilight Sphere hotel on her off days.

At first, she thought he was being kind. That's what angels did, right? They were good. Kind. Caring.

Sexy.

She crossed herself whenever she imagined Raze out of the business attire he habitually wore. He was beautiful in the face, if hardened and cold, but that body of his... he'd removed his suit jacket a few times, revealing a thin, white button-down molded to the most perfect torso she'd ever seen. His thighs were a thing of beauty, and that ass—

Unh.

But he was also so far out of her league, she couldn't imagine what he was doing, spending all of his time with her. She finally had to admit that while he *was* good and kind and caring in his gruff kind of way, Raze wasn't *nice*. Their dinners together weren't because he felt like he had to take care of her. The way he stared when he thought she wasn't paying attention wasn't part of their bargain.

And the single rose that arrived in a plain glass vase every morning just for her wasn't something he did for all the damsels in distress he saved—mainly because, the more she learned about the infamous Raziel, the more she finally understood why Ariel tried to talk her out of relying on the Angels of Sin City to help her escape her contract.

Raze only helped someone when he was getting something out of it. Almost as bad as one of the fae, he relished bargains, and he had no problem cheating to get what he wanted.

For some unknown reason, Raze seemed to have decided that he wanted *her*.

There was no denying it. Even for someone as oblivious as Becca—who had a habit of mistaking flirting as friendship, and true love as a pointless fling that lost her her soul—she finally figured out that Raze was claiming her as his.

The way he scared off Anthony the werewolf should've been the biggest clue. Or how he asked her after the first rose delivery if she liked his gift.

Nope.

It was one night, about two weeks after she first started working at the casino, when he stopped talking in the middle of his sentence only to lower his head and steal her lips in the faintest of kisses that Becca finally caught onto the fact that Raze—surprisingly enough—was into her.

It was a fleeting kiss, almost as if he was testing how she would receive his advances. And, sure, she had sworn that she would never fall in love again after what Gabe put her through, but this wasn't love. This was undeniable attraction and gratitude and a sexual chemistry that she'd been fighting to ignore since the moment Raze walked into the bar and she felt a punch in her gut.

It wasn't forever. If she was being honest, she doubted that his attention would last out her first month of employment. He was keen to keep whatever they had a secret, and Becca was more than happy to go along with it. While working under Lucifer, no one would ever accuse her of sleeping with the boss for extra benefits. Though their relationship hadn't gotten that far, she was damned if she'd ruin the good thing she had going now.

Just because the casino was called the House of Sin, it didn't mean she had to *act* like it really was.

Still, there was no denying the reality. Within a few weeks of meeting, she found herself dating one of the Angels of Sin City—and she'd never been happier.

Too bad it wouldn't last.

CHAPTER 7

I t took three weeks before Micah managed to corner him in the office and ask about Becca.

Rumors had been flying. Raze expected that once the other beings caught sight of the two of them spending time together. He almost thought Micah would ask after Raze accompanied Becca to the Twilight Nights Club last Saturday, but that was the night Sam finally—*finally*—made a reappearance so Raze dodged a bullet there.

Sam refused to tell them what he'd been up to which basically confirmed Raze and Micah's suspicions: whatever it was, it had everything to do with Polly Benson. Especially since, the next morning, he was gone again without so much as a "See ya."

But that was Sam for you.

Eventually, Raze began to think that Micah

guessed. And, based on his history with soulmates, he wasn't saying a damn word in case he jinxed it for his older brother. It would make sense, after all. The second he first met his witch, he shouted it from the rooftops that she was meant for him, only for her to disappear shortly after. He never found her again and, after forty years, Micah had long given up hope since even her coven had proclaimed her dead.

As it turned out, though, his oblivious brother had no idea. When he finally asked if Raze had decided to end his decades-long streak of celibacy with the new server, it was clear he had no clue that, instead, Raze was actually courting his soulmate.

His jaw dropped as soon as Raze begrudgingly admitted the truth before his light eyes shone with happiness for his brother.

"Are you fucking serious? That's amazing, Raze! When can I meet her? I want to welcome my new sister to the family."

His response wasn't that unexpected. Even though he was lost without his mate, Micah had the best soul of the three of them. He wasn't hardened like Raze, and he wasn't trying too hard to prove he was good like Samael. Nope. Micah was inherently divine, and the only reason he fell with his brothers was that he was too loyal to stay behind in Heaven in the first place.

"Not yet, Micah." As soon as he started to argue, Raze cleared his throat. "Look. She doesn't know yet, okay? I don't want to bring her around you guys until she does."

Micah's look of horror would've been hysterical if it didn't reflect how awful Raze was feeling himself. The further he took things with Becca without telling her one teeny, tiny detail—like, oh, she was his soulmate— the worse it got. Especially since there was a good reason she didn't quite know just yet.

"What are you waiting for? Don't you remember what happened to me? You need to cement that bond while you still have the chance!"

Though he never wanted to use Micah's story as a warning, he'd been telling himself the same thing for weeks. He could very easily lose Becca before their bond was finalized, but he was more worried about her rejecting him once she learned the truth.

He shook his head. "I want to. Trust me, I really fucking do. But I can't. I can't tell her now."

"Why the hell not?" demanded Micah.

"Because I spent the last three weeks making it clear that this was a temporary arrangement," Raze admitted bitterly.

His brother groaned. "Okay. And what the fuck did you do *that* for?"

"It seemed like the best idea at the time. You don't know Becca. She's... nice. Good. She believes the best in people. And..."

"And?" prompted Micah.

Raze huffed out a breath. "And she told me when we met that she swore off falling in love again. Bad history," he said before Micah could ask. Considering his brother knew all about that, Micah let it go. "But she meant it. I sensed the truth in her words then, and when she asked me if I ever found my soulmate, I lied. I fucking lied, Micah."

It was on one of their earliest dates, back when Becca hadn't even realized they *were* dating. She'd gone into a little more detail about her contract, and the fucking idiot of a human who she sacrificed her soul for. Gabe Watson bought ten years extra time after Becca made a deal with Lucifer to save her high school sweetheart, though he dumped her the second she had. It seemed fitting that he barely got to enjoy his extended life, and that he ended up in Hell anyway, the asshole.

But while he was being tortured, she was the one sentenced to an eternity of servitude to the devil himself. The way Becca told him of her time in the Pit, she'd gotten off easier than her ex-lover, but barely. What made it worse was that Gabe had certainly earned his place in Hell while Becca—his sweet, innocent Becca who wouldn't even swat a mosquito if it was biting her—only ended up down below because of her soft heart.

She deserved an eternity with a soulmate that worshipped her. Pity that couldn't be Raze.

He understood that. But Micah?

His brother couldn't.

"Tell her. What's the worst that could happen?"

"She could tell me that she doesn't want to be bound to me."

"True," acknowledged Micah, "but then you'd have closure. And maybe your demoness will surprise you. I mean, after everything I heard about the two of you together... it seems she's pretty into you. Go on. Tell her the truth. Then maybe you could claim her and you can ride her instead of my ass for a change."

He knew what his brother was doing. Like always, Micah was trying to lighten the mood, try to make Raze smile instead of his perpetual scowl.

If only it worked.

With a long, drawn-out exhale, Raze admitted, "I wish I could. But, for me, brother... a soulmate was never in the cards."

Micah's pale eyes lit up as he offered Raze a reassuring grin. "Hey. We run a casino, Raze. What is that but a house of cards?"

BECCA'S HEAD SNAPPED UP AS SOON AS SHE HEARD THE knocking at her door.

It had been bowed over her clasped hands, fingers probing the familiar beads of her rosary as she prayed.

It was the same routine she'd done every night before she prepared for bed: reflect over the day, moon over her growing feelings for Raze, pray that he wanted to stick around her just a little longer.

Maybe she was torturing herself. Apart from a few stolen kisses here and there, their... whatever they had... hadn't progressed at all. He still sent her roses every day, visiting her at the casino when he could, even told her during quiet moments on the rooftop that he loved her—a feeling she reciprocated but could never say out loud—but she could already sense Raze withdrawing.

He barely touched her anymore. If she brushed up against him, he jerked, then quickly moved away, even though she was the one jolted by his celestial aura. The few times she made it clear she was open to initiating sex, he quickly shut her down.

Something was coming between them, and though their relationship had been fleeting, she didn't regret the time spent with Raze. She only hoped that, when he moved on to the next damsel in distress, he didn't forget the deal he made with her in the beginning.

As soon as the first round of knocking ended, she hesitated, though she crossed the room before the second round finished. Flinging open her door, she was stunned to find Raze—still completely dressed in one of his full business suits—standing out in the hall.

Becca had changed from her uniform into an old,

comfy t-shirt and a pair of sleep shorts. Her hair was piled up in a messy bun on top of her head, her face clean of any make-up.

Her stomach dropped to see him so strikingly handsome as she stepped back, allowing him to stride royally into her room.

"Raze? I... did we have something planned tonight?"

He shook his head.

She hadn't thought so. Another reason why she'd been convinced that he was slowly ending what they had going on.

Since they met, no matter what he was doing, he usually found her on the third floor at the end of her shift if they were doing something together. And while she'd seen him every night this last week, when he didn't show up, Becca figured he was busy. After all, they didn't have to spend *every* free moment together. Just like how last Saturday he had passed the evening with his brothers, Becca assumed he had big, head of the casino, hotshot things to do.

Now that he was here, though? She had another sinking suspicion.

This was it, wasn't it? When Raze finally came to call things off.

Well, it was fun while it lasted.

Keeping her voice light, she said, "What's up?"

"I know it's late, but I just finished talking to one of

my brothers and, damn it, he was right about something. I had to come to see you and tell you. I'm sorry, Becca. It couldn't wait."

"That's okay," she lied. "Come on in. Sit down. Make yourself comfortable."

"If you don't mind, I'll stay standing."

Yup. Definitely not a good sign.

Honestly, she'd been expecting this ever since their relationship had spread amongst the rest of the casino staff. Becca didn't care; she could put up with her fellow servers' good-natured teasing with ease. But Raze was the boss, plus one of the angel princes. He had to be getting more grief that he was slumming with a demoness who worked for him. And though Micah had a good reputation, the fact that she'd never met either of Raze's brothers had been a huge, honking warning sign for Becca.

His brother was right? To Becca, that only meant one thing. Either Micah or Samael had made it clear to Raze that he was wasting his time with her. For the sake of their faction and their casino, they probably pointed out that it was better for the rest of them if he broke things off. And, from the look of things, Raze had agreed.

So, bracing herself for the inevitable answer, she asked softly, "What did you want to tell me?"

"I'm not sure how to do this, and it's going to come as a shock regardless, so I'm just going to say it."

Becca, we're over. "Okay."

"Becca—"

She held her breath, willing herself not to cry.

"—you're my soulmate."

Wait. What?

Soulmate?

CHAPTER 8

Becca's eyes went wide. "But... did you say 'soulmate'?"

He nodded.

Shaking her head, she whispered, "That's not possible."

Raze planted his expensive dress shoes against her floor, hands folded behind his back. His handsome face gave nothing away as he said, "I assure you, it is."

"No." Her voice rose a little louder as everything she thought she knew turned on its head in an instant. One second, she was expecting Raze to dump her. The next? "You don't understand. I'm a demon. I'm not one of Blane's subjects, either. I wasn't born like this. I sold my soul, Raze. I told you that."

She did. Becca made that perfectly clear from the beginning. Even when their early attraction turned into something *more*, she never once made promises to Raze that she couldn't keep. As his employee, she was more concerned with the power imbalance at play. He was one of the Angels of Sin City, with more power, money, and influence than anyone else Becca knew— save the cruel male who owned her soul with a contract she couldn't breach.

Years ago, she swore off being so impulsive. Swore off getting in over her head with charming males, too, but that was the thing with Raze. He wasn't charming. At first, he seemed cold and calculating, though Becca knew better now. He was loyal and protective, and— she had to admit—more jealous than she realized at first. But charming? Not even a little.

That was part of the reason why she allowed him to seduce her in his firm way. Because he never turned any charm on her, because he never pushed her further than stolen kisses and dinners out on the Strip when he guided her out of the hotel as her bodyguard, she thought he was just upholding his end of their deal.

Still. No denying that starting this... whatever they had... this *thing* with Raze had been an impulsive decision. Becca hadn't regretted it, though, even when her gratitude toward Raze easily turned into affection. She liked him, probably cared for him more than she should, but that was as far as she was prepared to take it. Eventually, Raze would turn his steely blue gaze on the next helpless damsel in distress, Becca would have to hope Lucifer was too distracted with his evil schemes to come after her, and the last few weeks in Sin City would be a distant memory.

That's all they could be.

So why was Raze coming to her *now* to tell her that she was his soulmate?

Becca wasn't exaggerating when she said it wasn't possible. Maybe if she'd been born a demoness like Ariel, serving the immortal demon king Pazuzu—though he went by Blane Puzu these days—then she might have believed Raze; born demons were more powerful than the demons Lucifer created, and they had a lifemate they spent ages searching for. When it came to Becca, though? Part of selling your soul to the devil was actually giving it away.

Lucifer owned her soul. Signed, sealed, delivered—she gave it to him years ago. And, without a soul, how could she be any being's soulmate?

Especially one of the royal angels?

And not just a prince, but *Raze*?

"So?" Raze raised his eyebrows, the only hint of emotion on his sculpted face. "I still have one. And, from the moment we met, my instincts have been telling me that you're it. You're my soulmate."

"I—" Becca was suddenly dizzy. Was the room spinning, or was that just her thoughts? "What does...

Raze, what does that mean? What do you want from me?"

"I want you for life."

"But you're immortal."

"Fair enough." He nodded. "Then I want you for eternity."

Eternity.

Becca blinked.

"I should've told you before, but I..." He paused, seemed to think over what he was going to say, then added, "I didn't. I didn't know how to tell you. I didn't know how you'd react. I hoped you'd take it well." A small frown as he watched her back away from him. "I'm not sure you are. What's the matter, Becca? Don't you want to be with me?"

"I—"

He hardened his jaw. "I love you."

"I... I know. You told me that already."

Raze waited. When she wasn't quick to repeat his words back to him, he seemed to stiffen further. "I know this is... unexpected. And I don't want you to feel as if we have to finalize our soulbond right now. I'm willing to wait for you for as long as it takes."

"Because I'm your soulmate," she said weakly.

He nodded. One single decisive nod.

She swallowed. "Even though I don't have a soul."

"The bond is there, whether you want to acknowledge it or not."

Could he sound any less enthusiastic if he tried? Becca bit back a laugh that, more than likely, was a sob. "And finalizing this... soulbond thing? What's that mean? Like, sex? You want to sleep with me, even though you've never even tried to do more than kiss me since we've been dating."

Through suddenly gritted teeth, Raze said, "All it would take was one time. The first time we fuck, you're mine. I needed you to understand that. But I'm not pushing you to do anything. I told you. I'll wait."

Well, that at least explained why he was always so much of a gentleman. For all the times Becca wondered if maybe he really was just watching over her, that he enjoyed her company but he wasn't really attracted to her...

"One time?"

Another nod.

"I— I'm sorry, but I have to go."

Raze didn't move. He stayed where he was, almost like his shoes were planted to the industrial carpet of her hotel room.

He never tried to stop her, only asked in a voice so icy cold it sent shivers down her spine, "Go where, Rebecca?"

Oof. Full name and everything.

She shook her head, already jamming her feet in her sneakers. "Out for air," she said. She didn't waste time grabbing her purse. Right then, she needed some space from Raze and his overbearing presence. "I'll be right back."

Did he answer her? Becca had no clue. She thought she might have heard him say something under his breath as she fumbled with her door, escaping out into the hall. It hit her that she was probably making a mistake leaving her purse behind. Her room key was in there, so she was basically locked out.

Later, she told herself. She'd deal with that later.

For now?

She needed that air desperately.

Once she made it outside, she gulped in a breath, then kept going. Her head was spinning, her feet carrying her away as if she could outrun Raze's confession.

It was only supposed to be a good time. She had repeated that over and over again these last few weeks if only because she was guarding her heart against further heartbreak. What happened with Gabe was so long ago, she hadn't remembered how much it hurt to care more than her partner—and now she was supposed to believe that Raze knew all along that this was more than a fling?

If Raze had told her in the beginning that she was his soulmate, it would've been like a dream come true. To find love and protection with the angel? To know that he was keeping her safe because of her and not because—as she believed—she'd made a bargain with him?

Maybe Raze didn't know her at all. Because if he did, he never would've kept the truth a secret.

That was the issue at hand, she realized as she pushed past happy couples, drunk tourists, and some pretty annoyed locals... it wasn't that she was his soulmate that had her running, it was that it took him all this time to actually *tell* her.

When a being found their lifemate, they pounced. Even for someone like Becca, born human and changed into a demoness, she knew that. What did it say about her that Raze was able to keep it a secret for these last few weeks?

Even worse, what made him change his mind?

He already told her he loved her. She hadn't really believed him at first, even as he sent her roses and stayed up all night talking with her. How could she? He could care for her, sure, but unless she was his fated soulmate, it could never compare to the feelings he would eventually hold for *her*.

And now he wanted to admit that she belonged to him all along?

She needed air, but she also needed to think. Only then, when her frantic thoughts could make sense of everything he told her, would she return to him and tell him that she wanted to be with him. To Becca, who had been satisfied with whatever time Raze was willing to give her, eternity was definitely a bonus.

Only... she just needed a second to fucking *think*.

And that's what she was going to do.

Even though she had spent one day a week tempting sinners in Las Vegas while she was still working out of the Pit, she usually stayed closer to the Twilight Sphere hotel if only because it was faction-owned. No surprise, then, that she got herself lost. Too busy running her last conversation with Raze through her mind, she kept going, not really having an idea *where* exactly she was heading to.

It wasn't until she made it about a half of a mile down the Strip that she realized her mistake.

The stink of rotten eggs wasn't too unusual, either because she was used to it during her time in the Pit, or because Las Vegas in the summer wasn't all that pleasant. She walked right into it, too consumed with thoughts about Raze and what she was going to do when she went back to the hotel to see him.

Now that the shock was wearing off, she had to admit that this was a bit of a relief. No matter how hard she tried not to fall for the angel, knowing they could never last, she'd only be lying to herself and everyone else if she said she wasn't already gone over him. What did knowing that she truly was fated to be with him forever do except ease her mind? Unlike Gabe, once she bonded to Raze, he couldn't leave her. It wasn't the way paranormal beings were wired. Nothing could change that.

Except not getting the chance to tell Raze that she wanted to be his bonded mate.

Becca didn't notice the stink of sulfur, or the heat that seemed to slam into her despite the late hour. But the ugly, bumpy, red-skinned fire demon with eyes like shiny marbles and black horns rising high over his spiky hair?

Yeah. No way she could miss *that*.

She strangled her gasp of terror and surprise when she glanced up and noticed that, somehow, she'd found herself on an empty stretch of road. No one else was around except for her and the demon she would've done anything to avoid ever seeing again.

He smiled when he knew he had her attention. Oversized fangs hung over his lips, making it seem more like a snarl, but she knew him. The scent of her fear did more to make him happy than anything else— except perhaps her screams—would.

"Jerroz. I... what are you doing here?"

Demons like Jerroz never left Hell. Even if most of the local humans knew about the factions that ran the City of Sin, they expected the beings to look some-what human-like. They could deal with things like Raze's angel wings, a vampire's fangs, or a fairy's pointed ears, but a fire demon? No way. Especially since the beings' laws said that humans weren't to be harmed, and a sight like this would be pretty damn harmful.

And that was even before Jerroz got his hands on them.

"I've been looking for you, Rebecca." Jerroz reached up, stroking one of the onyx horns jutting out of his mis-shapened brow. "No one leaves the Pit."

Quick as a snake, he used that same hand to lash out and grab her wrist. Careful to go for the one without the rosary, Jerroz pulled her into him, her flesh sizzling as he tightened his grip on her bare skin. A fire demon, he could control the burn, just like how he incinerated Simon. And while he didn't light her up, he made sure she *hurt*.

Though she didn't want to give him the satisfaction, she couldn't help it.

Becca screamed.

Jerroz laughed. "Ah, music to my ears, young demoness. I can't wait to hear it again once I get you back to Hell."

That was exactly what she was afraid of.

And, as Jerroz transported her away in the blink of an eye, there wasn't a damn thing she could do to stop him.

CHAPTER 9

A house of cards, just like Micah said. Only, unlike how his supportive brother meant it, the relationship he had with Becca must've been a true house of cards.

Flimsy.

No foundation.

Why else would she have run away like that?

No.

No.

Raze refused to fault Becca for her reaction. The only one to blame was him and how he never should've kept the truth from her in the first place. Then, after making it seem as if what they had was nothing but a quick fling, was he really so surprised that she didn't take the prospect of being stuck with his selfish angel ass for the rest of eternity all that well?

Yeah, right.

Raze gave her ten minutes. Ten minutes to be alone, to gather her thoughts, to, as she put it, "get some air". He felt pretty generous giving her those ten minutes, and if it was really only eight before he threw open her door and chased after her, who was really counting?

He raced toward the elevator, jabbing the button repeatedly until it finally arrived on the thirteenth floor. A pair of British vampires—leftovers from the vampire emissary from London who decided to stay in the City of Sin a few weeks longer—took one look at Raze, then politely exited the elevator so that the bristling angel had the car all to himself.

Since the thirteenth floor was closer to the ground than it was the penthouse, he went down. He figured it was the same way Becca would've gone, too, and if he needed to take flight, he could always launch from the sidewalk as easily as he could from the rooftop once he released his wings.

A part of Raze hoped that she would be right outside, waiting for him to come after her. He tried not to be disappointed when he was unable to spot her blood-red hair among all the tourists milling about, gawking at the skyscraper of a hotel. Even though they weren't officially bonded yet since he hadn't claimed her body and soul, Raze could still follow the tie between them to go after his soulmate. It was the same way he was able to always track her down anywhere in the casino during one of her shifts. He instinctively knew where she was.

She'd gone east. Hoping he could overtake her without resorting to his wings, Raze headed off in the same direction.

He'd gone about ten steps when, out of nowhere, the bond just... disappeared. Trying desperately not to dwell on just what that could mean, he shoved his trembling hands in his pockets, pushing past all the tourists meandering their way down the Strip. It was dark out, but like New York, Las Vegas never truly slept. Neon lights, headlights, flashing lights... he was able to see exactly where he was going.

There was no sign of Becca anywhere, no matter how far he went.

Raze's aura flared when he caught the hint of sulfur. Two street lights *pop*-ped as he stormed by them, his celestial aura catching them in the crosshairs. Glass shattered on the pavement behind him, but Raze didn't give a shit.

Though Las Vegas definitely had its days when it reeked, the scent of rotten eggs was so much worse— though maybe that's because Raze knew exactly what caused it.

Brimstone.

Becca was missing, and the path she had taken out

of the hotel intersected with a bloom of sulfur lingering in the hot air.

It didn't take a genius to figure out what happened —or an angel, either.

Raze stopped short, spinning around. With his angelic senses, he could just trace Becca to this spot. She might've gone a few steps further, but her innate aura lingered just under the sulfur. Worse, he recognized the nerves that tainted her essence.

Something happened.

Something not good.

Without even giving them the order, his wings burst from his back; good thing that he'd tracked Becca to an alleyway where no one else dared to tread or he might have clipped anyone standing nearby with them. He was alone, but that wouldn't be the case for long.

Whatever happened to Becca, he'd get her back.

Unless—

"Raziel."

Raze turned again, facing what had been a brick wall—an empty spot in front of a brick wall—only moments ago. As he did, he flared his wings at the familiar, cultured voice.

No one ever called him by that name; at least, not to his face. To use an angel's true name inferred that you held power over them. As the years passed, Raze refused to answer to anything except his chosen nickname. Even though it was common knowledge that his angelic name was Raziel, unless they wanted to risk his wrath, they stuck with Raze.

All except one former fallen angel, it seemed.

"Lucifer. What did you do with her?"

He hadn't changed one bit. From the goatee to the black hair slicked back into a tail, he enjoyed playing the part of a roguish businessman. Only, instead of dealing in dollars, he dealt in souls.

Bastard.

Unlike Raze, Lucifer currently kept his wings hidden. He wasn't surprised. Even though, when it came to the celestial beings, showing off your wings was akin to a dick-measuring contest, Raze knew that Lucifer never showed his off if he could help it. After spending so long in Hell, the black feathers that used to match Raze's had become leathery. Instead of fluffy angel wings, Lucifer's were ratty. Torn. Like a bat that got caught in a hailstorm, his wings were destroyed.

Just another reason why Lucifer hated Raze and his brothers almost more than he hated any of the other factions.

Though he wore a pleasant smile, Raze could see the loathing in Lucifer's icy blue eyes as he folded his hands primly behind him. "Why, Raziel. Whatever do you mean?"

"Cut the shit. Rebecca Murphy. Where is she?"

Lucifer tapped his chin with a perfectly manicured nail. Hard to believe this male could be cruel enough to trap his Becca, or vicious enough to curse those who crossed him, but that was what made him so deceptively evil.

"Rebecca, Rebecca, Rebecca... nope. Sorry. Doesn't ring a bell."

Lying. He was lying.

And there was nothing Raze could do about it without risking anything bad—*worse*—happening to her.

"Fine. If you don't know where she is, then what the hell are you doing here?"

"Hell..." Lucifer let out a soft laugh. His eyes remained cold and hard, though, without even an ounce of humor. "Funny you should mention that. I don't know. I guess it's nice to get out of Hell every once in a while. Don't you agree?"

"Don't know," spat out Raze. "Never been there."

"That's right. The Fallen linger in Purgatory. Can't get into Hell. Can't get into Heaven, either." His lips split again. "What if I could change that?"

Raze froze. "What do you mean?"

"It's very simple. For old times' sake, I'm prepared to offer you a deal." Lucifer held up both of his hands. They were folded into fists, hiding whatever was inside. Waving his left one, he said, "If you choose this, I'll give you what you need to go home." He unfolded his hands, revealing a shimmering image of the golden key Raze and his brothers had lost ages ago. "Heaven."

"What's in the other one?"

"If you choose this one, I'll sneak you into Hell with me. There might be something you want there." His grin turned devilish as he unfolded his right hand, revealing an image of a perfect red rose.

Becca.

Raze narrowed his gaze on Lucifer. "Alright. Let's say I bite. What would you want in return?"

"It's very simple, Raziel. If you choose one, you forfeit the other. *Forever.*"

For a moment, the temptation to choose the rose was all too real. Only knowing that this was Lucifer, and that the devil could never be trusted had Raze screwing his jaw shut as he thought about Lucifer's offer.

He wasn't a fool. He knew what Lucifer was doing. If Raze entered into a deal with the devil, his celestial side would hold him to it. He could choose the key, but he'd lose Becca. He could choose Becca, but his brothers would be sentenced to spend the rest of their lives in Purgatory.

And if he didn't have both his soulmate *and* their talisman, there would be no breaking the curse that Lucifer placed on his faction.

Besides, who was to say that Lucifer would honestly fulfill either offer? No one knew for sure where the key was, and he was holding out hope that Becca was safe. Even if it appeared that, by chasing after his demoness, he'd inadvertently walked into the perfect trap set by Lucifer.

Raze was sure of one thing: his soulmate would never set him up, especially for the lord of Hell. But Lucifer was crafty all the same. When Raze first met Becca, he had wondered if she was the perfect lure— and she was. She really, really was.

Lucifer knew it, too, which was precisely why Raze scoffed and said, "I'm good. Thanks anyway."

The devil shrugged. "Suit yourself."

Then, before Raze could demand Lucifer stop playing his games and admit he knew what happened to Becca—even though he was sure he already knew himself—Lucifer disappeared in a plume of black smoke, leaving a fresh wave of brimstone slapping Raze in the face.

Raze threw back his head, letting loose a bellow of rage that had car alarms in the distance blaring, before he spiraled up into the air, hoping that he hadn't just made himself a bigger cautionary tale than Micah ever was.

CHAPTER 10

Talk about déjà vu.

It had only been a handful of weeks since she first made her escape from the Pit, but nothing changed. There was her cubicle with its ever growing list of souls for her to enter into her computer. The black mark outside in the hall that was all that remained of poor Simon. And, of course, Jerroz leering as he detailed every inch of delicious torture that he was going to put Becca through for leaving her post.

When she was first planning on how to get out of Hell, it was this precise scenario that had her hesitating for so long. As a low-level demon, the endless busywork was bad, but it wasn't painful. It wasn't torture. If she betrayed Lucifer, she would be tossed to devilish demons just like Jerroz, a fate worse than simply dying.

It had all been worth it, though, for the chance to be free of this. She'd died once, her soul being relegated to Hell courtesy of her reckless agreement with the devil. She'd pushed herself to escape if only because the one thing Becca had wanted was freedom. Even if she had to die again, that was fine, so long as the endless monotony finally *ended*.

But then she met Raze. And even before he admitted what she—okay—probably knew all along to be true, she was glad she risked everything for the chance to get to know him. To love him. She had a second chance beyond her wildest dreams, but she threw it all away the second she went outside for some air and a moment to think.

And now that she was actually about to face some real torture? She couldn't help but think that nothing could be as bad as never seeing Raze again.

Jerroz must've picked up on how little his threats were affecting her because the ugly demon kept making the torture sound more and more frightening. She barely paid him attention which, of course, only incensed him.

Literally.

The Pit, already so hot and humid, started to fill with smoke as Jerroz started to lose his temper. She remembered what happened to Simon and, for a moment, understood true fear. But it faded almost entirely in the next. Maybe that was what she needed.

If she was looking at an eternity in the Pit, knowing what she could have had with Raze, what she gave up because she let her fear rule her, then maybe becoming a black scorch mark on the floor was another way out.

His burn from before had already faded. Even though it hurt like, well, *hell,* demons had a high tolerance for pain as well as a fast healing ability. If Jerroz wanted to, he could make the torture last and last— which was precisely what she didn't want.

A quick way out. If that's all she had left to look forward to, then that was what she was after.

She opened her mouth, ready to say something to goad him further when, all of a sudden, the last voice she'd ever hoped to hear again came lilting down the hall.

"Where's the girl?"

Jerroz stopped smoking at once. With a smug glance over at Becca, he dashed out into the hall, waving his hand over his horned head.

"Over here, my lord."

Well. Suicide by demon was looking a lot more promising than whatever Lucifer had in store for her.

She swallowed. Then, because she didn't know what else to do, she sat at her desk, running her rosary beads through her fingers as she waited for Lucifer and Jerroz to return.

The Pit was hot, but her beads were cool; even in

the depths of Hell, they provided both comfort and relief to Becca. She'd almost forgotten about that small quirk. Now, she clung to it. At least it was one small thing to keep her from losing it entirely her as her worst nightmares came true.

For such an evil creature, it was a shame that Lucifer didn't look the part. Like Raze, he had angelic good looks; only the pointed goatee fit her image of the villain he truly was. He exuded poor malice, though, his aura almost as black as his hair. He was bad, deep down to the depths of his rotten soul, and he reveled in that.

Just like he would revel in whatever consequences he laid on Becca for betraying him.

Jerroz was jabbering at his side. The demon hadn't seemed so short before, but seeing him come up to Lucifer's shoulder really made her notice how tall and imposing the devil really was.

She gulped as he strode into her cubicle, Jerroz saying, "I have plans for her, my lord, if you'd like to hear them. First, I thought I could—"

What it was the demon planned to do to her, Becca didn't know. Because, as soon as she was able to rip her terrified stare from Lucifer's expression, she noticed something glittering in front of his pitch-black shirt.

Hanging on a simple golden chain, she saw an elaborate-looking key. Bigger than would fit most ordinary doors, it was glittering gold and had an aura that was achingly familiar.

Lucifer caught Becca's stare. A smile that could only be called devilish tugged on his lips as he slipped the necklace beneath his black shirt.

And then he said, "That won't be necessary, Jerroz. After my little jaunt upstairs, I think this is exactly where I want the girl."

"But, sire—"

Lucifer's eyes swirled with red. Unless Becca was imagining it, it seemed like there were actual flames licking at his pupils.

Jerroz shut his jaw so quickly that the tip of his oversized fang sheared off a hunk of his tongue. It landed on the floor with a wet slapping sound.

Lucifer's smile widened. "As I said, that won't be necessary."

As the maimed demon nodded hurriedly as black blood spilled down his chin, Lucifer swept down the hall. Once he was gone, Jerroz ran down the hall in the opposite direction, leaving Becca alone in her cubicle.

Forget giving up. Now that she'd seen the talisman hanging around his throat—now that she was sure Lucifer *wanted* her to see it—Becca refused to sit back and wait around for Jerroz to take his sadistic pleasures out on her.

She couldn't stay in the Pit. She *couldn't*. Who knew how long Lucifer's faux pleasantry would last, and she was sure that the only reason Jerroz hadn't already stopped to retaliate was that he was concerned with Lucifer lopping off more than a bit of his tongue.

But what to do?

She glanced down at her wrist as if drawn to it like a moth to a flame. It was risky, but there was only one thing she could think to do.

Whether it was because she'd inadvertently spent decades imprinting on the rosary, or because of the tattoo she had etched into her skin in this life and her last, Becca was a bit of an oddity in the Pit. Though she was a demoness, she still considered herself a practicing Catholic. She had faith in the rosary, almost as much as she had in her feelings for her angel.

He protected her when he didn't have to. No matter what she had to do, she would make sure to do the same for Raze.

There were times in the Pit when, despite the overwhelmingly swampy nature of the heat, her rosary was like a salve against her skin. No demon, regardless of their level in the hierarchy, ever attempted to take it from her, mainly because no one but Becca was brave enough to touch such a holy relic. There was still some magic in the beads, and as it chilled her to the bone, she wondered if being so close to Raze these last few weeks had done something to charge it.

She'd always wondered if there was something about her rosary that would help her break free of

Lucifer. Too afraid to ever try, Becca figured that this was the only chance she had.

If it worked, she could get back to Raze.

It better fucking work.

Thinking of her angel, remembering the hard shape of his jaw, the cool look in his steely blue eyes that warmed up whenever he watched her, the reluctant smile she'd caught maybe once or twice... remembering the surprise she felt to hear she was his soulmate, followed by the strange sensation that it... it was *right*... remembering how he made her safe, made her *whole*... Becca closed her eyes and prayed that she could get back to him.

And, leaving her beloved rosary behind as a token of her sacrifice, she miraculously made her escape.

———

IT JUST ABOUT KILLED RAZE THAT, AS A CELESTIAL BEING, he wasn't allowed to enter Hell.

Just then, on the heels of Lucifer's flashy disappearance, he would've given up his last claim to Heaven if only he could drop further down below and get to his soulmate.

Did he blame himself before? If so, not enough, because this was *all* his fault. If he'd told her from the beginning that they were fated to be together, this never would've happened. Becca wouldn't have felt betrayed that he kept it from her for so long, and she wouldn't have run out of the hotel where Lucifer had been waiting to scoop her up and take her back to the Pit. Almost as if he'd witnessed her abduction himself, his angelic senses assured him that's what happened.

Damn it!

It didn't matter that Lucifer offered him a choice, either. Raze knew him well enough to know that this— all of it—was some kind of trap. Lucifer wanted to make him squirm. Raze was willing to bet that he never would've upheld either side of his bargain. He was just after getting Raze to admit what was more important: the talisman or his soulmate.

The talisman would lead him back to Heaven. Becca would make Heaven on Earth for Raze.

Both of them would lead to Lucifer's curse being broken, but of course the devil left out *that* detail.

Still. It didn't matter. If Lucifer knew anything about what it was like to have a soulmate, he never would've made his laughable offer.

The answer was Becca. It would always be Becca. And though he was sure Lucifer knew that otherwise he wouldn't have gone to such lengths to get to her, Raze never would've given him the satisfaction of hearing him admit it.

The second Lucifer was gone, though?

He took to the skies, venting his frustration while praying that somehow, some way, the Heavenly Father or one of his lost brothers would hear him and help him find his soulmate. He searched, though he knew it was pointless, and he cast his aura like a net on the odd chance that his weakening powers would do *something*.

He didn't have the faith that it would. Millennia of living among the mortals beat the last of his hope out of him, turning him cold, turning him cynical—until he met Becca. Raze didn't know what would happen if he lost her so soon after finding her, but considering the way Micah closed off after the death of his witch, he worried for the rest of the City of Sin.

If he couldn't get Becca back, there might not be a city standing when he was done.

Just when he started to feel some of his aura eke out of his control, Raze thought about ending his flight before he realized he couldn't. He *couldn't*. Even if it was only for the one night, returning to the hotel was like giving up. Like accepting that Becca was gone out of his reach. And while that was true, he refused to believe it.

Hours into soaring over the Strip, fury keeping him aloft even as his wings tired, Raze kept going. When he could've sworn he felt a tug low in his gut, he couldn't dare let himself believe what that could possibly mean.

Still, his instincts had him wheeling around. Just in case.

And there, stumbling down an empty street on the outskirts of Las Vegas, her red hair wild and the stink of sulfur covering every inch of his soulmate, he saw her.

Rebecca.

Right as he arrowed his body and his wings toward the ground, almost in disbelief that their bond had almost subconsciously led him to her, he breathed in deep.

Fire and brimstone had never smelled so fucking good before.

As if she could sense him flying toward her, Becca stopped, staring up at the sky. When she let out a soft sob that carried on the wind, he knew that she saw him. He righted his body just before he touched down on the asphalt, snapping his wings behind him as he threw open his arms in time for Becca to fling herself at him.

As soon as his arms closed around her, Raze shuddered out a breath.

Suddenly, all was right in his world again.

Raze didn't know how long he held onto her. All he kept thinking was that it was a good thing she was a demoness since a mortal female would never survive the way he squeezed her to him, unable to let her go just yet.

It was only when he swore he heard her voice over the thump of his racing heart that he finally realized that she was trying to say something. Her words were muffled against his chest as she buried her face into him, arms thrown over his torso as she clung to him. Raze still wasn't ready to loosen his hold on her, so he didn't, though he did lean back enough so that he could understand her.

When he did? He almost couldn't believe it.

"Your talisman," she repeated. "Your key. I know what happened to it."

Her grey eyes glittered with something he couldn't quite place. It wasn't fear and it wasn't nerves, but it was... something.

And then Becca dropped the bomb:

"Lucifer stole it. Raze, he has it."

CHAPTER 11

Now that she'd escaped the Pit for the second time, Raze was desperate to bring her back to the safety of the hotel and then never let her out of his sight again.

One plus side to making their home base in Sin City? Most mortals had some contact with the factions in one way or another. They were more of an open secret than anything else, and while he'd have to be more careful if he lived in a heavily human-populated area, he didn't even think twice before he released his wings again.

It was the first time Becca had seen him with his full wingspan on display. She immediately marveled over them, calling them beautiful as she reached with hesitant fingers to stroke his nearest feather. He preened under her touch, enjoying it as she grew bolder, more confident in her caresses.

The time for pretending as if she wasn't everything to him was over. So what if she was a demoness and he was an angel? So what if she worked as a server in his casino? He'd give her his shares in the business if she wanted him to, he'd serve alongside her, he'd hand her everything so long as she took his soul, too.

There was no rush. He could wait for her to grow used to the idea of being his fated mate. Whatever it took—just as long as she was with him.

"Hold on tight, Becca, baby," he murmured, pressing his hands to her back so that she was against his body. "We're going home."

She didn't argue. Instead, hopping up and wrapping legs around his torso, Becca tucked her arms under his as she clung to him.

It was the first time they flew together, and with Becca so close, he vowed that it wouldn't be the last. For now, though, he just wanted her where he could keep her out of harm—and Lucifer's—way. The Twilight Sphere was his target, and he didn't stop flying until he'd landed easily on the walkway in front of the hotel to the surprise of more than a few tourists.

After disappearing his wings inside of him, Raze brought her to his suite—but that hadn't been his first destination. As soon as he led Becca through the entrance of the Twilight Sphere, he loaded her into the nearest elevator and jabbed his pointer finger decisively on the number '13' key.

Thirteenth floor. Becca's personal hotel room.

He had her tucked into his side, almost as if afraid that, if he let her go, she'd disappear on him again as they rode the elevator together.

She'd only been gone for a few hours but, to Raze, it seemed like a lifetime. Lucifer's sly offer still rang in his ear, and if he hated his old enemy before this night, that was nothing compared to how he felt now knowing that Lucifer had to have been lying in wait, specifically hoping to scoop up Raze's soulmate. Not because he owned her soul, but because it belonged to Raze.

He had to have known. Becca hadn't, but Lucifer must have—probably going back as far as Becca's contract, he had known.

Talk about playing the long game. Add that to Becca's reveal that Lucifer stole their talisman so long ago—that he purposely allowed her to catch sight of—and he knew this was about more than just the latest curse.

Raze had underestimated Lucifer once before. He wouldn't do that again.

Just like he wouldn't underestimate his soulmate.

During their flight, when he had asked Becca how she escaped, she showed him her bare wrist.

The rosary was gone. She'd used it, plus her faith

in Raze, to momentarily break the hold Lucifer had on her in order to escape the Pit, she explained to him over the rush of his flapping wings against the night's sky.

But it wasn't just that, Raze decided as he soared over the City of Sin. During the weeks they'd gotten to know each other, Raze's powers might've continued to wane courtesy of Lucifer's curse, but the bond stretching between them was more than enough to break Lucifer's hold on her.

Becca believed that she didn't have a soul. She was wrong. From the moment he found her waiting for him at that high-top table, he unwittingly gave her his.

No.

He didn't *give* it to her. It had always *been* hers. As his soulmate, he was only returning it to its rightful owner. Everything he was, everything he ever would be, was Becca's, including his soul.

And an angel didn't belong in Hell. When Raze and his brothers fell, they fell to Purgatory, and if that's where he had to stay, he would, so long as he had Becca with him. She was his everything, and he'd do anything he had to to make his dishonesty up to her.

He might not have told her from the beginning that they were meant for each other, but now she knew—and she still came back to him. Not because she needed him to protect her from Lucifer, either. With his soul nestled deep in her chest, Lucifer could try to claim her again, but he'd fail. Raze was certain of that. Whatever the lord of Hell stole from Becca, he could keep. She didn't need it, not when Raze's soul was more than enough for both of them.

That didn't mean he wanted to push her, especially after what happened to her. For too long he'd been putting his own needs first. It was time to respect what Becca wanted, which was why he made the move to bring her back to her room. Then, when she refused to step out onto the thirteenth floor, instead murmuring for him to bring her up to his suite, Raze realized that he was making the same mistake again. Instead of asking her what she wanted, he was deciding for her.

And that had to stop.

So he asked. He asked Becca what she wanted to do now, and listened when she told him that she wanted to take a hot shower, and that she didn't want to be alone.

He could handle that.

Becca didn't know what surprised her more: that her protective, overbearing angel had actually *asked* her what she wanted to do instead of telling her, or that when she admitted she wanted to wash the stink of sulfur off of her skin, he led her to his private bathroom—then closed the door behind her, leaving her all by herself.

Hadn't she made it clear when she told him that that was exactly what she *didn't* want? It didn't matter that only a few hours on Earth had passed since Jerroz captured her, dragging her back to the Pit. Or that she'd been the one to run out on Raze in the first place. Something about nearly being trapped in Hell again put things into focus for her.

So Raze forgot to mention that she was his soulmate until after they'd been dating for a few weeks. It took Gabe two years of dating before he uttered "I love you" that first time, and Becca had still been willing to sell her soul for that idiot. From the beginning, Raze had been nothing but devoted, even if he was also jealous and possessive, too. Call her sadistic, but she adored that about him. Finally, Becca felt like someone actually cared about her, and now that she knew it was fated?

Mate bonds did that to faction males. She'd be more worried if he told her that she was his soulmate, but he couldn't be bothered with her. It was the opposite with Raze. When they were together, she felt like she owned him. Which, admittedly, was a pretty heady sensation for an old maid and a low-level demoness.

An angel didn't just want her. He wanted her as his forever mate, bonded together so that no one could ever separate them. And if Becca had given in to her instincts to jump his bones instead of running out on him earlier, she could've avoided everything that happened after she left the hotel.

Then again, if she hadn't, she never would've discovered the truth about Lucifer stealing Raze's key. She considered that a small win, even if she had sacrificed her mother's rosary to learn it, but at least she had some small way to make it up to Raze after she got back to him.

But that was only the beginning. Though she hadn't been trapped long, the way just thinking of Raze gave her the strength to escape again made it clear what she had to do. He wanted to give her forever? Then Becca wanted to take it.

There was only one way to do that, though. It's why she pointedly told Raze that she didn't want to be alone.

How could she claim him as her soulmate when he was on the other side of the door?

Raze had already confessed once before that he found her to be his biggest temptation. He'd never taken it further than that, mainly because he was respecting the pace that Becca set. Now she knew the truth: if he seduced her in return, if he slept with her, he'd bond her to him for eternity.

So he didn't. It would've been so easy, too, but Raze wouldn't until he finally could tell her that she was meant for him.

Well, he was meant for her, and it was time she finally used those tempting training classes she was forced to go through for good.

Peeking her head out of the shower, she raised her voice so that he could hear her over the spray. "Raze? Where are you?"

"Here."

He sounded close, but she didn't see him. "Where's that?"

"Just outside the door, waiting for you to finish up in there. I thought we could order in some room service when you're done."

Becca bit back her sigh of relief. That, at least, was a good sign. He could've really abandoned her, but he hadn't. Instead, he was as close to her as he could get without intruding.

Well, damn it, she wanted him to intrude! Because she was hungry, but it definitely wasn't for food.

She wanted Raze.

"Can you come in here?" When he stayed quiet, she said, "Door's open."

She never locked it. One part of her had hoped that he'd follow her inside, while the other must've known that—if he didn't—she would call for him anyway.

She held her breath as she waited. A heartbeat later, the knob turned, the door pushing open.

And there he was.

He'd already shrugged off his suit jacket. His dress

shoes were most likely at their place by his front door. His socks were gone, leaving him in his button-down shirt and his slacks.

Perfect.

From experience, she knew that he would've dropped his phone, his wallet, his keys onto a dish in the front room. Therefore, she mused, there wouldn't be anything to ruin once she pulled the shower curtain back enough to crook her finger and gesture him closer.

Raze quirked an eyebrow, but he did as she requested. "Yes? Is there anything I can get you?"

What a gentleman. Though they both knew she was naked inside of the shower, his steely blue gaze stayed locked on her dripping face as she leaned out of the stall. A few stray droplets landed on his white shirt, immediately turning the spot translucent.

He wasn't wearing an undershirt, Becca noticed. Good. That would make undressing him all the easier.

It had to be this way, she realized. As much as Raze said that she tempted him, he'd spent the last few weeks treating her like an innocent virgin. But she wasn't. She was a demoness, and maybe she'd been celibate ever since Gabe broke her heart, but Raze remade it for her.

He wanted her to wait until she was ready. Well. Look at that.

She was.

Slowly, slowly, she pulled the curtain back. Then, when even her gentlemanly angel couldn't resist getting an eyeful of her wet, naked body, Becca grabbed him by the lapels and yanked him into the stall with her.

Raze was an angel. More than that, he was twice her size. No way she could drag him anywhere he didn't want to go. So even though she pulled him fully dressed into the shower, she knew that he had no arguments since he came along willingly.

Still, she peered up at him. With a coy smile as she lowered her hands, reaching for the first button on his shirt, she said, "I told you I didn't want to be alone."

Becca watched his Adam's apple bob as he swallowed roughly. "You did."

"And now you're soaked."

He never took his eyes off of her tits as he nodded. "I guess I am."

"I can fix that for you, if you want."

"What I want?" He shook his head, though he kept on staring. "It's not about what I want. And Becca, baby, you can do whatever the hell *you* want with me. I told you, I'm yours."

She was glad to hear it.

After pressing a quick kiss to his jaw, Becca went to work on his shirt. She undid his buttons, peeling each half of his drenched button-down shirt away from his sculpted chest.

He didn't say a damn word. He just let her, even helping her by shrugging off the last of it when the soaked sleeves got caught on his wrists.

While Raze did that, Becca reached for his slacks. A quick flick of the button had his pants springing open, the echo of the zipper being drawn down finally enough to rip Raze's eyes from her chest.

They locked on her face. "Becca. What are you doing?"

"Isn't it obvious? This is a shower, Raze. I'm wet. You're wet. I'm naked, so now I'm getting you naked."

"Yeah?" His voice lowered an octave as he brushed a damp strand of hair away from her cheek. "And then what? I wash your back, you wash mine?"

Becca smiled as she started to tug down his boxers. "You'll see."

The soaked material clung to his skin. She was just beginning to think that this seduction might have been better in the bedroom instead of the shower when Raze suddenly offered a hand. With a rough shove, he yanked his boxers down past his balls, revealing an erection that had Becca momentarily stunned.

Only momentarily, though. Because the second she saw that thick, long cock pointing toward her, she knew that she'd made the absolute right decision.

She'd always used to love shower sex. Something told her it would be even more memorable with Raze.

Her voice went throaty as she said, "You're still not naked, Raze."

"Guess I'm not," he grunted, reaching down to pull off the rest of his drenched pants. He made quick work of them before adding his boxers to the growing pile outside of the stall. "There. Now I am. You want to pass me the soap?"

"Not yet," she said, turning around. "Actually, I think we should get dirty first."

"Becca?"

She swallowed, hoping like hell that her attempts at a seduction were enough, before she said boldly, "Claim me."

"What?" The word came out strangled. Probably not the best sign. "Becca, I—"

Too late to turn back now.

"Please, Raze." She went up on the balls of her feet, bracing her arms against the tile as she lifted her ass. She was achy and empty, and now that she got a glimpse of that gorgeous cock, she absolutely needed it inside of her.

Peering over her shoulder, she saw the way he stared at her ass. A pained expression crossed his face as he reached down, gripping his cock at the base. He gave it a quick stroke, a rough one, almost as if he was willing it to behave.

He didn't blink. He just stared, his lips darting out to

catch a stray drop of spray at the corner of his mouth. With his free hand, he shoved his water-darkened hair out of his face as if the few damp curls were blocking his view.

He shuddered, but he made no move to slip his cock inside of her wet and waiting pussy.

"If this is because of Lucifer," he began.

She shook her head, wet hair slapping against her back. "It's not."

"Becca—"

"Use your senses. You know I'm telling the truth. I want you. I've wanted you from the moment you walked into the bar, but I never... I never thought you'd want me."

Raze moved into Becca, bracing his body over hers. He blocked the shower spray, but the heat from his skin, plus the nudging of his searching cock between her ass cheeks had her flushing with desire.

"I've never wanted anyone more," he whispered huskily in her ear. "But this is for eternity. I fuck you, I can't take that back."

She pushed back against him. "Good. 'Cause I don't want you to."

Raze's low groan gave her hope. Reaching behind her, she gently tapped his hand before slipping her fingers under his. Becca took control of his cock, positioning the head at her entrance.

"Take me," she murmured into the echo of the

falling spray. "All you have to do is push. Take me, and I'll always be yours."

Raze tilted his head so that he could take the edge of her earlobe between his teeth. With a tiny nibble that sent shocks of pleasure through Becca, he said, "Don't you get it, my mate? You always have been."

And before she could say anything in response to that, Raze did exactly what she told him to.

He pushed his cock to the hilt inside of her, stretching her to her limits with his girth. And it hurt. Sure it did. Becca hadn't had sex in decades, and even then Gabe was no comparison to Raze's inhuman size.

But it didn't matter. Because the moment he entered her body, the two becoming one, the pleasure of their soulbond snapped into place drowning out any ache from her protesting body.

Turned out that Raze was right after all.

They really were fated to be together.

CHAPTER 12

Raze kept his arm slung over Becca's bare shoulders, fingers buried in her tousled hair, face turned so that—even in bed—he had his eyes on her. He couldn't help it. It was as if the bond stretching between them kept him tethered to her side.

He'd lost her once. Though she'd made her way back to him, Raze still hadn't been able to soothe the possessive beast clawing away inside of him. For the first three days after they claimed each other as mates, he couldn't even bear to let her out of his sight. Only when Becca pointed out that they hadn't left his bedroom in days, and that she'd like to wear something other than one of Raze's button-downs or his sheet, did he entertain the idea of letting her head back to her room.

And even then, when he finally admitted she had a point, he accompanied her back to the thirteenth floor and helped her pack. Now that they were true soulmates, he expected them to live together. Since his executive suite was much bigger than her hotel room, she accepted his offer to move in with Raze on the upper floor.

Cute, he had thought as he shouldered her luggage for her. As if he wouldn't have found some way to convince her if she said 'no'.

It wasn't about whose room they stayed in, either. It was having her close. Raze would sleep on the streets of Sin City if that was what his soulmate wanted, and he'd do it with a smile.

His lips quirked at just that thought.

Raze's angelic senses picked up on sudden surprise mingled with affection. He could feel it pulsing down their mate bond, so he knew he was catching Becca's emotions.

He thought she was still sleeping. Considering he basically fucked her into unconsciousness last night, she should be.

It was Raze's fault, and a badge he'd wear proudly. After they returned from packing up her belongings and bringing them back upstairs, he promised that he'd help her put it all away after dinner. They ordered in from the Twilight Bar & Grille, Raze ignoring Zev's knowing smirk as the werewolf owner of the bar brought the room service up personally. Considering the way the wolves gossiped, he was willing to bet that Anthony told Zev and Dev all about how Raze staked his claim on Becca long before he ever admitted to another soul that she was his true mate.

But, instead of going through her suitcase, Becca dragged Raze to the first floor of the hotel once they were finished eating; so long as she stayed inside of the Twilight Sphere, he was content to follow her anywhere. After showing Raze off to a giggling Ariel, Becca bought a dozen cupcakes from Rhea down at the Twilight Sweets Bakery for dessert.

Since she hadn't seemed so keen to start unpacking, Raze figured it could keep until morning. Instead, he carried Becca back to bed with him until she—exhausted from pleasure—finally fell asleep. He slung one possessive arm over her, tugging her against his naked body, and just enjoyed the connection he shared with his soulmate.

He must've fallen asleep at some point because he was feeling quite refreshed. He was, he noticed, also completely erect. No matter how many times he had taken Becca over the last few days, he was hard again almost immediately after he finished. For the first time in millennia, Raze couldn't shake the lust—and with his demoness having a sexual appetite to rival his, he didn't have to.

His eyes were closed. Slowly, he lifted his lids.

Had there ever been such a splendid sight to wake up to?

My Rebecca...

Even though she was lying flat on her belly, her head was turned toward him the same way that his was to hers. Her deep-red hair was tucked over her left shoulder, arms crossed as they pillowed her chin.

She was staring at him. A curious look in her lovely grey eyes, her lips parted slightly.

That was the surprise he sensed washing over him. The affection was like a gentle caress—an emotion he noticed not too long after Becca came to work for the casino—though it became undeniable from the moment he first claimed her; one good thing about his lingering angelic senses, he decided, since he didn't have to waste time wondering if she cared as much as he did. She did, and Raze made it a point to tell her as often as he could that he felt the same way.

When it came to the factions and their lifemates, they put the human's vows of "'til death do you part" to shame. Now that she bonded herself to him, Becca was his—and he was hers.

"Hey." His voice came out gravelly and rough. Slowly, he untangled his fingers from her hair, stroking the column of her throat. "Morning."

As his fingers moved over her skin, she shivered slightly. "Morning."

She was still staring at him.

Raze ran his fingers over the curve of her shoulder. "What?"

"It's just... I don't think I've ever really seen you smile before. Not like this."

For a moment, his hand stilled. And if he just so happened to freeze right as he was touching the swell of her bare breast, well... he was still a *fallen* angel. No one had ever tempted him more, and now that *she* claimed *him*, he was more than happy to give in to that temptation.

Raze thought about what she said. The shock in her soft voice, the hint of shyness that lingered even as she boldly shifted her naked hip, nudging his aching hard-on.

To be fair, Becca wasn't wrong. The responsibility to House of Sin and his brothers had weighed so heavily on his shoulders over the last few decades. Taking care of Micah, making sure Sam didn't get himself into trouble... heavy was the head that wore the crown. Raze was a royal angel, the leader of his faction on Earth, and smiles were a luxury he couldn't afford.

Then again, so was a mate. Even before he found his true soulmate, the most he could hope for was one-night stands.

Now? Now he was looking at spending his very long, very immortal life with his Rebecca. Not even Lucifer could separate them since Raze shared his soul with Becca. Let the lord of chaos claim her human side. If she didn't mind calling a rogue angel her mate, then he was more than happy to claim a demoness as his.

And she was. For now and forever, Raze would have his soulmate to rule at his side.

His smile deepened as he eased his hand further down, splaying it against the small of her back. His fingers curved over the edge of her hip, shifting her closer to him. When the head of his cock prodded her right side, she turned slightly, opening her body up to him.

She wondered why he smiled now? As Becca lifted her leg, placed it over his as Raze guided his cock to her entrance, it was a wonder that it took her this long to notice.

"I'm happy," he said honestly, pushing his cock inside of her. "I've never been so fucking happy in my life." Bottoming out, he shuddered as Becca moaned, gripping him tightly. "And if you keep doing that, I don't think I'll ever stop smiling."

She squeezed him. "That gives me something to work toward then," she promised. "I like it when you smile."

He worked himself in and out of her a few times before gripping her gently, rolling her with him until he was flat on his back and she was on top of him. Raze was so used to being in control. With Becca, though?

He discovered that, if only with his mate, he relished letting her have all of it.

"Ride me," he said, more of a beg than a demand.

Leaning forward, she swiped her tongue over his nipple. It was hard, the sensation enough to tear a guttural moan from his chest. Right before he could go on and plead with her to do that again, Becca started to move, and Raze was barely able to form coherent thoughts other than, "Oh my fucking *God*, that's good."

You think he'd be used to it by now. For the last few days, Raze and Becca stayed inside of his—now, *their*—suite, cementing the mate bond stretching between them. Between sharing their bodies in bed and more of each other's life story whenever he could bring himself to give her some time to rest, they were becoming what they were always fated to be: soulmates.

Right after he first claimed her, Raze got in touch with Micah, letting his youngest brother know that he had his soulmate back, that he had claimed her, and that he planned on spending the next week or so mating her at every opportunity. Micah was in charge, and he'd bring Becca down to the casino to meet him officially as soon as he could.

Sam, on the other hand, was missing again. No surprise. Micah admitted that he had stopped in, then took off again while Raze was going out of his head, searching for Becca. As of yesterday evening, he was still out of contact. Micah wasn't worried, so neither was Raze. Their brother was probably on another crusade to prove that he was more than an ex-angel of death, like always.

At least, that's what Raze thought—until a banging could be heard coming from the front of Raze's suite right as the sex started to get really good.

Becca immediately stopped moving. Since that was absolutely unacceptable, Raze gave her a playful slap on her ass. "Don't stop. If you love me at all, you'll keep going. *Please*."

Pressing her hands against his lower torso, using Raze's toned body for leverage, she lifted her body up before dropping down on him again.

"That's right, my mate." Raze reached up, tweaking the nipple nearest to him. Not enough to hurt, but enough to send a jolt of pleasure through her. Becca threw back her head, the pure ecstasy reflected in their bond, as she rode him harder. "I love you, too."

He'd been the first to say the words, and he said them at every opportunity. From the moment he first shot his seed inside of her, the second the bond snapped fully into place, he figured there was no reason to keep it back, even if it wasn't the first time he actually said it.

Raze told Becca he loved her quite often, and if Becca was still hesitant to repeat the words, that was okay. After all, they were just words, and as much as he tried not to remember that she'd loved before him, it wasn't like he didn't have a past, either. For now, it was about their future—and for both of them, there would never be anyone else.

So he could wait. Especially since he could feel her love for him with every beat of her heart, every panted breath as she fucked him with everything she had.

"Raziel! Open this door."

Becca didn't stop, but she did raise her eyebrows at Raze as soon as Sam's bellow ripped through their bedroom.

He didn't stop there.

Bang.

Bang.

Bang.

"Me and Micah gave you three days to fuck your mate. So wouldja get your cock out of her pussy for five damn seconds and answer the fucking door?"

Raze was going to kill his brother. He often took off for weeks at a time and *now* he decided it was the perfect opportunity to demand to see him? Raze made sure to pass the message along to Micah that, should Sam show up again, Raze was busy with his new mate. Anything else could wait.

Anything.

Too bad it didn't seem as if Sam had gotten that message.

Huh. Looked like he was going to have to kill Micah, too.

Just in case Becca got any silly ideas, he gripped her by her waist, guiding her to continue riding him; he didn't want to stop just because Sam had the worst possible timing, and he prayed that she didn't, either. Not that he would ever force his mate to do anything she didn't want to. Raze was content to give her full control—even if he thought he'd explode if she left him like this.

Still, he waited a moment to see if she was willing to keep on fucking, and when she squeezed his cock again, he knew that she was.

Thank God.

"My brother can wait," he told her, making sure to lift his ass enough to increase the friction between their bodies. "If that's okay with you."

With an impish grin, Becca dug her nails into his skin. "I'm close," she admitted.

In that case—

"Then Sam can fucking wait until I get you off," Raze promised. "Hang on, Becca."

"Oh. Oh! *Oh...*" His soulmate gulped, her grey eyes sparkling with desire. "Okay."

EPILOGUE

He was as good as his word.

When Becca's pants became shorter, her nails leaving tracks near the dips in his hips, Raze took control.

Flipping her over, he slipped his hand between their slick bodies, rubbing her clit in measured circles that became more and more frantic as he pounded away inside of her.

Only when her pants became soft moans did he know that she was about to come. He'd learned that his soulmate was a bit of a screamer, but she was staying as quiet as possible as if she hadn't forgotten that Sam was lurking out in the hall.

His brother stopped yelling when he realized that Raze was going to come out when he was good and ready. Already annoyed at Sam's unexpected intrusion, he hated that Sam stole Becca's screams of pleasure from him. Promising himself—and his mate—that he'd make it up to her, he swallowed her next moans in a deep kiss as she finally came around his cock.

He let himself climax as soon as he was sure that Becca was satisfied. Then, because he was still pretty pissed at Sam, he kissed her sweat-slicked forehead, nuzzled her nose, nipped beneath her jaw as Becca got her breath back.

For a moment, he thought she might have finally forgotten about Sam; if she had, Raze had no problem leaving Sam out there all day. But after she had recovered from the way he worked her body, she shoved his body off of hers. Raze landed on his back with a soft *oof*, letting his petite soulmate manhandle him any which way she wanted to.

He had a momentary hope that she was ready to climb on top of him again. Those hopes were dashed when she scampered off of the mattress, giving him an enticing glimpse of her behind before she crossed the room, zeroing toward the suitcase Raze had left on his couch.

"Come back to bed," he murmured. "I already miss you."

"Can't." She yanked the zipper open, ruffling around the clothes stuffed inside, pulling out a few pieces at random. At least, it came off as random to

Raze. Becca, on the other hand, seemed to know exactly what she was doing.

But it wasn't lying on her back, legs in the air as Raze went down on her, so he wasn't sure why it mattered.

"Why not? I'm horny."

Choking on a laugh, Becca pointed out, "I'm beginning to realize that you're always horny."

When it came to her, that was very true.

"I waited a long time for you, Becca."

"And you can wait a few minutes more. I've got to get dressed."

She shimmied on her silk panties. Raze had to swallow before he started to drool. Wouldn't be sightly, the angel prince leaving a pool of saliva on his sheets.

Instead, he propped his head on his hand, his elbow on his pillow as Becca gave him a show. Once she had her panties on, she started to pull on a pair of jeans that sculpted her delectable ass. She jumped in place to get them on, making her tits jiggle.

So enchanted by that sway, he forgot for a moment that she was in the middle of covering up.

"What for? Don't get me wrong, Becca. I'll peel your clothes off of you with my teeth if you let me, but I'm already naked. I want you naked, too. Come on. Come back to bed."

"Raze!"

"Yes?"

"Your brother," she whispered.

She must've realized that her shout of his name had echoed, most likely catching the attention of said brother, and she was lowering her voice.

Oh, yeah, Raze thought. Definitely going to have to kill Sam, especially if his annoying presence was the reason why Becca was getting dressed instead of joining him in their bed again...

Hm. Maybe if he pretended like he didn't know what she was talking about, she really would forget about Sam.

It was worth a shot.

"Yeah? What about him?"

"He's still out there, right?" Becca pulled on her bra, quickly doing up the hooks behind her. Grabbing the first blouse she saw, she yanked it on over her obvious bedhead. "He's still out there. I want to meet him."

Of course she did.

Raze exhaled roughly, casting his eyes toward the ceiling before he reluctantly climbed out of the bed.

Whatever Becca wanted, Becca got.

Scowling—not at her, never at her—Raze found a pair of faded jeans in his dresser before stabbing his legs through them. He didn't bother doing the button or even grabbing a shirt or shoes. Proclaiming himself dressed if only because his still wet, still hard, still aching cock was concealed, he waited until Becca pulled on her sandals before he led her toward the front door.

He could sense his brother's celestial aura through the wood. There went any hope that Sam had a lick of shame, that he left the suite until Raze was ready to see him.

When Sam finally claimed his soulmate, Raze decided, he would make sure to return the favor. So what if the brothers were thousands of years old? Sibling rivalry was alive and well in the House of Sin.

With a huff, Raze waited until Becca was standing beside him before he flung open the door.

"Finally, I—" Sam's jaw clamped shut when he noticed Becca right next to Raze. His dark eyes flickered over her—relief brightening them when he noticed she was fully dressed—before he nodded. "Rebecca, I assume?"

"I'd hope so," she said sweetly. She held out her hand graciously. "And you can call me Becca."

Sam took her hand, shaking it quickly before hurriedly letting go. His gaze danced back over to his brother, careful not to get too close to Becca.

Smart angel. There was a reason why Raze purposely kept his brothers from meeting Becca at first —and it had nothing to do with Becca, and everything to do with the possessive nature of a bonded male. Turned out, it wasn't just shifters that felt the bizarre need to claim their mates. Angels were very much included in that mix.

No wonder Sam was so focused on saving that human thief of his.

Speaking of—

"What are you doing here?" Raze demanded. His first round with Becca had only taken the edge off. He was still hard, plus he was hungry. For breakfast, for a taste of her pussy... Raze wasn't picky. He just needed to get rid of his brother first. "I thought you were busy."

"Not as busy as you, Raze," quipped Sam. He pointed at the open button on Raze's jeans, then wiggled his fingers at the obvious bulge pushing up against the zipper. "Sorry for interrupting."

"Like hell you are." Raze snorted while Becca hid a giggle behind her hand. "Whatever. You needed something?"

"Well, yeah. If you'd picked up your phone at all last night, you'd know."

Raze had purposely ignored its incessant ringing. He hadn't taken more than a single night off from running the House of Sin since it opened back in 1953. Sue him for wanting a few days to honeymoon with his soulmate now that they were bonded.

"I left Micah in charge of the casino. If he needed anything, you could've helped."

Sam was already shaking his head. "It's not about the casino."

Oh? "Alright. I'll bite. What's so important that you had to interrupt me and my mate? Because, I'm telling you, Sam, if the casino's not burning down, then it had better be good."

"It's the talisman."

Next to him, Becca went still. Raze didn't blame her. The last anyone mentioned the angels' talisman, it had been Becca telling him she caught sight of it hanging on a chain around Lucifer's neck. She sacrificed a lot to come back to Raze to tell him what she knew about it—and then she turned him into the most blessed male alive when she bonded with him.

Lucifer's curse made it very clear. If the three leaders of each individual faction found their talisman *and* their mates, his curse would be broken. But coming so close on the heels of Becca seducing him —*choosing* him—without him suggesting that she should, he was leery of hanging his hopes on the talisman.

Not that he didn't want his powers back. A return trip to Heaven... sometime after meeting his soulmate, Raze decided that an eternity with Becca in Purgatory was better than going back to a place that hadn't wanted him in millennia and all because he sided with Lucifer once upon a time, then lost his key.

But it wasn't lost, was it? It was stolen by his old enemy, a fact confirmed by both Becca and Lucifer.

So what did Sam know now that Raze didn't?

"Tell me," he ordered.

Becca moved into Raze, gripping his upper arm lightly. He could sense her nerves returning as she watched Sam, waiting for his answer.

He'd known her for a handful of weeks, a blip in the time they would eventually share together, but already he could tell what was going through that gorgeous head of hers. Now that the curse was common knowledge—as was the way to break it— Becca was probably wondering if he only agreed to bond with her because claiming her as his soulmate was one step toward regaining his power.

He wanted that power. Raze wasn't going to deny that. Probably not for the reason she was thinking of, though. He wanted to be strong to protect her, to keep her close, to make sure that no one ever had the chance to rip her away from his side again.

And to do that?

He needed his faction's talisman.

He needed that key.

"Sam," he prodded when his brother's gaze landed on Becca again. "What about the talisman?"

"Oh. Right. The talisman. I know where it is."

"So do we—"

"*And* I know how to get it."

Well, that was new.

"What? Really? How's that?"

Sam cleared his throat, a strange expression

twisting his features for a second before he banished it. It was a dark look, Raze noticed, but he knew Sam better than he knew most beings. The look wasn't for Becca, but what she represented.

Which was why he wasn't the least bit surprised when Sam said, "We're gonna steal it from Lucifer. And I have just the thief in mind..."

AND THERE YOU GO!

While this is the end of Raze and Becca's story, there's still plenty to come as the angel princes work toward breaking Lucifer's curse, finding their soulmates, and regaining their powers—not to mention, the key to the pearly gates.

Up next? *Ace of Spades*, featuring the middle brother, Sam, and his human soulmate (and notorious thief), Polly.

Keep reading to get a peek at the cover as well as the description for the second book in the *Forged in Twilight: Royal Angels* series!

Samael is not what anyone expects. Least of all himself...

Because Sam is a rarity among fallen angels — he's a self-professed guardian angel with a taste for death. Back before he and his brothers fell, he was considered an angel of death who ferried souls to Heaven and Hell. Now that he's been trapped in Purgatory for millennia, he lost the title, but not the instincts.

Determined to prove that he's moved on from his old life to his new one as one of the owners of the hottest faction-owned casino in Las Vegas, Sam has relied on his snow-white wings to rehab his image. He's no longer an angel of death but, instead, a guardian angel who does good deeds for the hell of it — all while Raze cashes in on the favors in the name of the angel princes of Sin City.

And then he meets Polly and, for the first time in a long, long time, Sam doesn't just play the part to spite the Heavenly Father. He actually wants to save her — especially since he met the adorable human while she was attempting to steal from House of Sin, their infamous casino.

She almost pulled it off, too, which would've been enough to catch Sam's attention. Then there's the undeniable fact that he instantly recognized her as his fated soulmate before she cheekily made her escape.

But there's no escaping Death when he's got his sights set on you...

When Raze and his new mate get a lead on where to find their missing talisman, Sam makes Polly an offer she can't refuse. Ten grand if she can retrieve the key for him, twenty if she lets him tag along on the mission. And while Polly might be a human, she'd been around the factions long enough to know that having a guardian angel at her back couldn't hurt.

Especially one as irresistible as Sam.

* *Ace of Spades* is the second novella in a PNR trilogy featuring three strong and sexy angel princes. Cursed

by Lucifer and banished from Heaven, the trio of fallen angels have to find their soulmates and track down their missing talisman in order to break their curse and get their HEA. *Ace of Spades* is the story of Samael and Polly, a guardian angel of death and the wayward human he'll do anything to save.

Out now!

AVAILABLE NOW

WANT TO READ A DIFFERENT TAKE ON THE FALLEN? CHECK OUT TRUE ANGEL TODAY!

Halo or horns?

Humans look at Camiel and think that he's an angel... until his black wings unfurl and it's all, "*Oh, no! Demon!*"

Yeah. Not quite.

Cam is an Othersider. Which, okay, just means that he'll eventually be one of the two... just not yet. Formally known as the Fallen, Othersiders walk—and, yes, sometimes fly—among the humans, knowing that their every step, their every move, their every *thought* adds to their tally. If he's good, he'll finally earn his halo.

If he's bad...

He's working damn hard to resist any urges to be bad.

It's a good thing he has his auditor at his side. Dina might look like a neighborhood stray, but it's the cat's job to help Cam get the points he needs to go from Fallen to Angel. And it's working... until Cam meets Avery.

Avery is human, she's in trouble, and Cam decides that she needs her very own guardian angel. If he can help her save her sister from the feral shifter that ran off with her, then maybe he'll finally prove that he's a good guy.

If only it was that easy. Because Othersiders? There's a reason why they're stuck on Earth, working hard to prove where they belong: they're cursed.

So when it comes to falling in love? There's one rule.

Don't.

Now Cam is losing his feathers at an alarming rate. In the middle of his mission, Dina disappears. Avery is a temptation he can't ignore, and when he doesn't, that's when all hell breaks loose.

Literally.

True Angel *is the first in a new series by the author of the* Claws Clause. *Think* The Good Place *but set on Earth,* *where every action means our hero is one step closer to earning his halo or his horns. And when he meets his fated mate, he realizes that he'd take either if it meant that he could have her by his side for all eternity.*

Out now!

STAY IN TOUCH

Interested in updates from me? I'll never spam you, and I'll only send out a newsletter in regards to upcoming releases, subscriber exclusives, promotions, and more:

Sign up for my newsletter here!

By signing up today, you'll receive two free books!

ABOUT THE AUTHOR

Jessica lives in New Jersey with her family, including enough pets to cement her status as the neighborhood's future Cat Lady. She spends her days working in retail, and her nights lost in whatever world the current novel she is working on is set in. After writing for fun for more than a decade, she has finally decided to take some of the stories out of her head and put them out there for others who might also enjoy them! She loves Broadway and the Mets, as well as reading in her free time.

JessicaLynchWrites.com
jessica@jessicalynchwrites.com

ALSO BY JESSICA LYNCH

Welcome to Hamlet

You Were Made For Me*

Don't Trust Me

Ophelia

Let Nothing You Dismay

I'll Never Stop

Wherever You Go

Here Comes the Bride

Tesoro

That Girl Will Never Be Mine

Welcome to Hamlet: I-III**

No Outsiders Allowed: IV-VI**

Holidays in Hamlet

Gloria

Holly

Mirrorside

Tame the Spark*

Stalk the Moon

Hunt the Stars

The Witch in the Woods

Hide from the Heart

Chase the Beauty

Flee the Sun

Curse the Flame

The Other Duet**

The Claws Clause

Mates*

Hungry Like a Wolf

Of Mistletoe and Mating

No Way

Season of the Witch

Rogue

Sunglasses at Night

Ghost of Jealousy

Broken Wings

Born to Run

Uptown Girl

Ordinance 7304: I-III**

Living on a Prayer**

The Curse of the Othersiders

(Part of the Claws Clause Series)

Ain't No Angel*

True Angel

Night Angel

Lost Angel

Touched by the Fae

Favor*

Asylum

Shadow

Touch

Zella

The Shadow Prophecy**

Imprisoned by the Fae

Tricked*

Trapped

Escaped

Freed

Gifted

The Shadow Realm**

Wanted by the Fae

Glamour Eyes

Glamour Lies

Forged in Twilight

House of Cards

Ace of Spades

Royal Flush

Claws and Fangs

(written under Sarah Spade)

Leave Janelle*

Never His Mate

Always Her Mate

Forever Mates

Hint of Her Blood

* prequel story

** boxed set collection

Printed in Great Britain
by Amazon

82960738R00096